NEVER GO BACK

A 'BIG DAVE' THRILLER FROM THE ALEX KING SERIES

A P BATEMAN

Facebook: @authorapbateman
www.apbateman.com

Rockhopper Publishing

ALSO BY A P BATEMAN

The Alex King Series
The Contract Man
Lies and Retribution
Shadows of Good Friday
The Five
Reaper
Stormbound
Breakout
From the Shadows
Rogue
The Asset
Last Man Standing
Hunter Killer
The Congo Contract
Dead Man Walking

The Rob Stone Series
The Town
The Island
Stone Cold

Standalone Novels

Hell's Mouth

Unforgotten

Short Stories

The Perfect Murder?

Atonement

Further details of these titles can be found at www.apbateman.com

For my Mum
My most avid reader, naturally...

ONE

Fiji

THE AUSTRALIAN STOOD in front of him, the machete in his right hand and the talisman in his left. It was swinging from side to side, like a hypnotist's pendulum, and he had a gleeful look in his eyes. He was close to the cliff edge. Five-hundred feet below him, the surf crashed on the rocks. There were few places with a break in the reef surrounding the island, but this was one of them. Two miles out, and separated by three miles of ocean, feathers of white water sprayed in the air as twenty-foot rollers peeled off and crashed down on the outer reefs and ebbed away in the lagoon. But here, on Devil's Leap, the southern swells funnelled between those two reefs and unleashed their power at the foot of the cliffs with all their fury.

"End of the road, Lomu," the Australian said, looking over the big Fijian's shoulder to where his companions had managed to regroup, some bloodied from the gunfire, but most with a look of vengeance on their faces. "You're a big, tough guy, but you'll never take us all at once."

"Maybe not. But I'll take you," Lomu replied and carried on advancing. Six-four, eighteen stone and unafraid. He wiped blood from his brow and looked the man in the eyes. "You're a murderer. And you'll get what's coming to you..."

"I guess you could do with a weapon right now," he said, making a show of the machete in his right hand.

"Don't need one. How about I ram my fist in your mouth and rip out your tongue?"

The Australian watched the second pickup slew over the loose surface, great rooster tails of dust and gravel thrown from the rear wheels. The sound of the V8 engine caught up with them, but Lomu did not look away. Unseen, four men leapt from the bed of the truck, shotguns in their hands and the crew that had got here first were bolstered by the reinforcements and started to shout and jeer. "It's over," he said.

"The hell it is..."

"They'll be in range in a matter of seconds. They'll be able to shoot you without hitting me, and then we'll toss your body down into the sea and the sharks will do the rest. Nobody will ever find you, and nobody will care..." The man paused. "Your family have done without you for almost twenty years, I doubt they'll even notice you're gone."

Lomu quickly checked around him, then looked back at the Australian. He had beaten the odds all his life. He had left the islands when he was just sixteen. A British armed forces recruitment ship had anchored offshore like something out of the slave trade two hundred years before and whisked him and his friends off to a 'better life'. Samoa, Fiji, the Seychelles – young men had been recruited and sailed back to Britain signing their life away to the Royal Navy or the Army on the voyage to a damp, cold and unfamiliar country that they would promise to serve, but never quite call home. Pay scales had been better in those days for the longer period a recruit signed up for and Dave Lomu, later known by his fellow soldiers as 'Big Dave' because of his huge stature and voracious appetite for both food and the opposite sex, had signed his life away for the full twenty-two years. He had travelled the world, but never back to his native Fiji, and he had fought and bled in Afghanistan for three long tours. Cut loose after sixteen years of service through budgetary cutbacks and the general downsizing of the British armed forces, Lomu had fallen into security and later worked as a bodyguard. The wrong time and wrong place had seen him seek employment on the mercenary circuit where he met the same faces in the usual countries where mercenaries plied their deadly trade. One such contract had led him to work as a deniable asset for MI5, and he had later been employed officially by them for two years. He had no idea where this unofficial sabbatical left him with Britain's Security Service, and nor did he care. He was here because family mattered, and he had been away too long.

The Australian tested his shoulder with his fingertips, where blood seeped from a bullet graze. At least one of Lomu's bullets had found its mark, against all odds during the car chase. For some reason Carter had used his right hand, and not the left in which he held the talisman. The machete was heavy, and the blade wobbled as the man tested the wound. The blade blocked his view for a moment, but as with things that mattered, it was a moment too long. Lomu lunged as the thick blade blocked the man's view of both him and the gathering of men behind him.

Leading with his left foot and dropping his right knee, Lomu's righthanded straight punch caught the man in the solar plexus, and his fist went around two inches deep, crushing the bone and driving the wind from his lungs. Carter dropped the machete and fell backwards, but Lomu snatched the talisman and for a second, all that stopped the man from falling was the thin leather necklace in his hands. Lomu snatched it backwards and Carter teetered on the precipice, his arms flailing wildly, before he fell backwards into the abyss.

The gunshots started at once, and Lomu felt the sting of hot lead shot on his legs as he snatched up the machete. He had nowhere to run, nowhere to hide. He could see Carter sliding down the slope below him. Not quite sheer, but certainly impossible to climb down. Risking a glance, he saw the men reloading their double-barrelled shotguns as they rushed forward to a more acceptable range. Fiji's gun laws were strict and despite its military and police being armed with the latest and greatest hardware, civilian ownership was down to shotguns and some hunting rifles with only registered collectors licenced to hold anything else. But a shotgun was as deadly as it gets when the range got down to forty metres or less, and the men were as near as damn it, deathly close.

Lomu stuffed the talisman in his pocket as he leapt over the precipice and slid down the shale cliff-face on his back-side and used the machete as an oar to both slow and control his descent. It didn't work as planned and he was soon racing at a terrific speed, and perilously approaching the sheer cliff-face two-hundred feet below him. Using all his considerable strength, he dug the machete blade in deeper and the shale spat out rocks and earth in protest, the machete blade sparking like it was being hammered in a forge, and his descent slowed considerably.

His cargoes were shredded, and he could feel the loose rocks tearing at his skin. Above him, a volley of gunfire sounded like a military salute as the men fired two barrels and reloaded as quickly as they could with shaky hands and a belly full of nerves. These were not soldiers, and nor were their weapons effective now that Lomu had slid far from range. He could no longer see Carter but had missed the man going over the edge. With the visible curve of the slope disappearing before his eyes, he dug deeper with the blade, then shot forwards quickly as the blade snagged and broke in half, a metallic ring of protest filling his ears. All he could do now was hope, and as he went over the abyss, he held his breath and closed his eyes instinctively, wishing he had never answered the texts and calls, nor boarded the two-stop, thirty-six-hour flight that had brought him 'home'.

TWO

Nadi Airport, Fiji
48 hours earlier

DAVE LOMU HAD TRAVELLED LIGHT. He wore just a linen shirt, cargoes and his sockless feet were in just light-weight trainers that had taken the toll of the journey and smelled like three-year-old Parmesan Reggiano, and within a minute of stepping out of the air-conditioned airport and into the bright sunshine and humidity, he was almost soaked through with perspiration. He carried only a small backpack, but already knew that he would need more cloth-ing. And he needed to burn the trainers, too. The air was hot, and the sun baked the top of his head, his wiry afro cut short with clippers and shaved at the sides. His dark skin glistened with beads of perspiration and as he stalked along the pavement, he undid most of the buttons on his shirt, his well-toned abs and chest showing through as the shirt billowed in the breeze.

His shoulder ached. The cabin pressure had caused his

recent injury to swell and seep, and a small bloodstain had flowered on his shirt, but the swelling was reducing, thanks both to landing and the two Ibuprofen he had blagged from the woman seated beside him for the last leg of the journey. He pressed his fingers against the dressing and took advantage of the space around him to gently and tentatively circle his shoulder. The muscles were stiff and protested, and it was only when he increased the movement, that he felt the injury twelve inches lower and right over his top rib. Again, the wound seeped and he knew that the stitches and skills of his surgeon had been tested during the thirty-six hours of cabin pressure. He fished another couple of Ibuprofen out from his pocket and swallowed them down with the remainder of the plastic bottle of water, which was now the temperature of a ten-minute old cup of tea.

He would have checked his phone, but the battery was dead. But he figured he would simply pace back and forwards waiting to spot his lift, his muscles grateful for some use after thirty-six hours sitting on a plane, broken merely by two, one-hour stops. He had no idea what time it was, but he wasn't hungry. The airline had contained and controlled the passengers with out-of-sync mealtimes, and he had smiled and chatted up two of the cabin crew for extra meal trays and plenty of drinks to occupy him on the flight.

Lomu watched the Suzuki four-by-four swing in, clip the kerb and bounce perilously close to tipping. He hated the little 'jeeps' and had once rolled one around Marble Arch trying to outrun the police after a night's heavy partying with his regiment chums. Not his finest hour. He glanced at the woman in the driver's seat and noted that the steering wheel was on the right, just as in the UK. Strange that he had not remembered, but he had left the country before he had been able to drive. Lomu had reflected much on the flight and realised that he didn't feel like he fitted in anywhere. To white people he was simply black, but to Afro-Caribbeans his aquiline nose hinted at something else. Indeed, Fiji's gene pool pulled from the India subcontinent, Pacific Oceania – most associated with the Hawaiian people who started out from Fiji and Samoa - and of course there were the ubiquitous African slaves who had been used to cultivate the land to sugarcane fields and increase the white European empires. Lomu had travelled with the British Army and never settled in Britain permanently, and now, as he stood in the country of his birth, he realised that he was never going to feel at home here, either. Before leaving, his friend had told him, *"You can't go home again. Whatever you expect from returning home after a long absence, it's never the same. Nostalgia is a bitch."* His friend had credited the novelist, Thomas Wolfe, but had later conceded that it was only the first sentence, and he had added the rest, but Lomu had got the picture. Whatever he was going to do here, the trip down memory lane was going to be a bumpy ride at best.

"Get in," the woman said. Lomu looked at her and frowned. Bumpy ride? Here was the first pothole to jar him. She had only been ten years old when he had left. "You *gonna* keep your cousin waiting, bro?"

"Delilah?"

"The same."

Lomu realised that his mouth was agape. "You've grown..."

"That's what happens. Try coming home more than once every twenty-years and it may not be such a surprise next time."

"Still got a smart mouth," he said, as he tossed his

backpack in the rear and sat down heavily in the passenger seat. The tiny off-roader sunk down on its springs and his elbow dug into his cousin's side. "Where's Marie?"

"Working. She'll be home in an hour." She paused, looking at the blood on his shirt. "What happened to you?"

"Injury in the workplace," he replied.

She shrugged like she didn't care, which she probably didn't, and she put the car into gear, and they took off rapidly. After three-hundred-metres Lomu could tell that she didn't obey road signs, speed limits or the general rules of the road. Nor perhaps, even the laws of physics. They weren't even guidelines. She didn't use the clutch as it was intended either and grated the downshifts when she used the gearbox to slow instead of the brakes. As for the vehicle's poorly perceived road handling abilities, she was certainly living life on the edge. "What the hell is that smell?" she commented in disgust. Lomu shrugged. "Jesus, Mary and Joseph! It's your damned feet, man!"

Lomu crossed his ankles, and the smell only became more noticeable. He looked up and said, "Here, pull over..."

Lomu leapt out of the vehicle and walked across the short grass verge to a wooden shack selling beach shop tat and ice creams. He found what he wanted, paid the young boy behind the rickety table and walked back to the car, where Delilah stared at him, bemused. Lomu kicked off his shoes and Delilah made a gagging motion and laughed. He put the flip-flops on and tossed the shoes out of the vehicle as she pulled away.

"Hey, that's littering!"

"You want them in here with us?" She shrugged, conceding the lesser of two evils. "They'll come in handy for someone," he said.

"Yeah, if that *someone* wants to keep the flies away..." She paused. "Anyway, you sound funny."

"Funny?"

"Yeah. Like you're still *Island*, but a bit *EastEnders* as well. We get EastEnders out here on cable. Do you watch it?"

"No."

"Oh..."

She seemed disappointed. It was probably the only thing they were going to have in common and she'd been shot down. "So, what have you been doing?"

She shrugged. "What, yesterday, last week, or for the past twenty-years?"

There was a sting to the way she had said it. When he had left, it had been sudden and an opportunity to lash out at his family. When his father had died, he had lost everything. His role model, his friend, his future self. How can a son carry on without making his father proud? Of course, he learned that he could, but at the time he could not see it as possible. Losing his father was bad enough, but his mother had soon remarried and that only soured the memory of his parents as a couple, and a family. Lomu had kicked back hard against it. There had been family arguments, fights and the typical paths disgruntled teenagers took to self-destruct their present rather than construct their future. Hindsight is a wonderful thing, but Lomu could now see that he had been out of control and the recruitment ship hadn't so much been the lifeline he had needed, but a solid one-fingered salute of protest to his family. It was only recently that he realised that life had simply gone on for his family. There would have been outrage and sorrow, and some members of his family would have missed him dearly, but he had been too full of rage and anger to see that, and his stubbornness had not only robbed him of a family but changed everything for the ones he had left behind.

"Tell me about yourself."

"You first," she replied curtly. "Marie said you joined the army. What's wrong with the Fijian army? You had to go to the other side of the world? There's been enough *coup d'état* here to keep a solider busy."

Lomu knew about the government overthrows, but he had always assumed that little would change. There were so many cultural factions and identity problems that a stable Fijian government was always going to be unlikely, and the country had the most firearms per capita in the world, thanks to its military ratio over civilians. Given that civilians had little access to firearms other than shotguns and single-shot hunting rifles, Fiji was far from an oppressed state. The military served the people and thought nothing of removing an unpopular government before the electorate cast their vote. "I ran away from my problems," he replied.

"Lucky you."

"You have problems?"

"*Everyone* has problems. Some of us just stay and face them."

Lomu shrugged. "How's mom?"

"A bit late in asking, but she's doing OK."

"And Josefa?"

"You care?"

She had a point. His mother's second husband could rot for all he cared. He had once shared a unique relationship with the man, as one would have an uncle. Josefa had taught him to fish, to box, to dive for lobster in the lagoon. In his adolescence, the man had readied him for girls and talked him through sex and relationships, but all that had ended when his father had died, and Josefa had almost immediately taken up with his mother. "Just getting the background." Lomu paused. "It's been a while."

"Well, if you want to know how Josefa is; then you can ask him yourself." Delilah swung the tiny 4x4 off the road and they slewed on a gravel track. Lomu grabbed the rollbar and she laughed. "You're a lousy passenger," she said pointedly. "So, what have you been doing all these years? Marie didn't tell me much about you."

Lomu watched the sea glisten on the horizon as they skirted the coast, then started to head inland on the gravelled track. The track was gaining in elevation and soon they joined a tarmacked mountain road, the track clearly being a shortcut. The mountains were a series of extinct volcanoes that had once shaped the island. They were rocky, and both patchy and dark with one-time lava rivers that had flowed across the landscape and set to create natural barriers in the landscape. Intersecting these, were patches of lush vegetation and below the mountain road sugar plantations cut a uniformed swathe through what looked like jungle. The air should have been cooler here, but it still felt like an oven. "I served in the army, then joined the SAS," he said, quietly.

"What's that?"

He smiled incredulously. "Special forces," he replied.

"What's so special about them? And what does SAS stand for?"

"Saturdays and Sundays," he said trying to keep a straight face. He had forgotten that people in normal circles may not know. And when you don't know, you just don't know. "We only worked on the weekends..."

She shrugged, apparently uninterested. "I work at the local tourist information," she said. "I get paid to upsell diving trips and water sports excursions."

Lomu nodded. He knew how important tourism was to the Fijian economy. Part of the reason he was here by all accounts. He had barely thought about the other reason. He just hoped it would all pan out before he got too heavily involved, but he doubted he would be that lucky.

The view of the beaches below them may well have been on another island for all the familiarity he felt. There were large hotels and lodges, but the place seemed to have escaped the high-rise domination of other tourist places like Mexico, Greece or the Spanish Costas. There were now fewer palms, more roads and from what he could best guess, ten-times the number of buildings. Further out to sea there were many speedboats and parasails, windsurfers and jet skis. From what he had heard the surfing industry had swamped Fiji in the twenty-years since he had left and tours offered boat rides to the outer reefs and tiny islands for the truly competent surfers, as well as something called tow-ins, where an experienced jet ski rider would tow the surfer into waves so that the surfer could get an early start without paddling. He had seen something on ESPN where surfers rode giant waves in Portugal and had earlier pioneered the practice in Hawaii. Many surfers did not have the budget associated with tropical, long-haul travel, and so budget lodges and boarding houses had sprung up which also accommodated the hardcore traveller and gap year student.

"Where are we going?" Lomu asked, suddenly aware that they were far from the family home, and he had merely been settling in to enjoy the view.

"Where we think it happened."

"How do you know?"

"The earth and mineral content on the body. It's the only place on the island where the dirt is a match."

"How old was he?"

"Fifteen."

"Did you know him well?"

She shrugged. "You know how Fijian family works. You can't have forgotten about that, even if you've forgotten about all of us," she replied acidly. She pulled the vehicle off the road, and they bounced along a rough track. This time Lomu resisted holding on.

"I'm here, aren't I?"

"Yes, I knew him well," she snapped. "His death was a blow to all of us."

"And the girl?"

"Your sister."

"Half-sister," he corrected her. He did not know the girl, had never even seen a picture of her. She was Josefa's girl, and he had not been able to process that his mother would carry another man's child, let alone start a whole new family. From what Marie had said at the time, Lomu knew the girl to be fifteen years of age. Around the same age he had been when he had lost his beloved father and Josefa had been waiting in the wings.

"Still missing," she said curtly. "And her name is Monique."

Lomu nodded as he watched the track ahead of them narrow considerably, palm trees on either side of them, low-hanging fronds swiping the windscreen. They emerged suddenly and unpredictably into a clearing, a tremendous vista of the ocean before them, and the highest cliff imaginable separating them from an inconceivably high drop. He had never been up here and wondered why. The view was magnificent. "The police searched the area?"

"Of course. They called in the army, too. They used helicopters and dogs to search the area and the police called in civilians as well. Nothing was found. Only Mustafa's body."

"What sort of kid was he?"

"Mustafa was a good boy," said Delilah. "He was from a good family and now he's gone."

Lomu nodded. He got out of the vehicle and looked around him, taking in the silence and the spectacular view of the ocean. He looked back at Delilah, who had got out of the Suzuki and was walking around the bonnet. "What was the cause of death?"

"Blunt force trauma," she replied, taking a breath to steady her nerves. She looked ashen, her milky-coffee complexion draining somewhat. Delilah's parents were both Fijian, but whereas her father was Lomu's mother's brother, her own mother was from both Indian and European descent. Delilah had taken much of the European genes on her mother's side and instead of the tight afro hair of Lomu's family, she had straight, dark brown hair and the most invitingly kind hazel eyes that no doubt would melt a few hearts, if they hadn't already done so. "They basically smashed his head in with something smooth and hard. Like a cricket ball, or the end of a baseball bat, although the coroner discounted that as it was not spherical enough to cause such indentation."

"They?"

She shrugged. "We're convinced it's the consortium."

"And what do the police think?"

"They haven't even questioned them," she replied. "Any of them."

"But they searched for the girl."

"Her name is Monique. And she's *your* half-sister..." Lomu nodded. He should have been more sensitive, but twenty-years later it still hurt, and he saw his mother and

Josefa's relationship as a betrayal to his father, even though his mother had now been with Josefa longer than she had been with his father. She stared at him and said, "Do you not feel anything? She's your half-sister and she's missing. The last person she was with was found battered to death. What the hell is wrong with you?"

Bitterness, stubbornness and distance. Lomu figured all three would be about right. He had turned his back on his family, and he had never met Monique. He had wanted to a few years back but hadn't known where to start and the fact that he would never have been able to visit without seeing Josefa had put him off. He had just finished his final tour of Afghanistan and been cut loose by the British Army and thought the time might be right to mend some bridges, but he hadn't seen it through. The subsequent years drifting from close protection work to that of a mercenary hadn't been what he'd considered to be his finest, nor proudest of moments, even though it was ultimately to be mercenary work that had eventually led him to his employment with MI5. He looked at his cousin and shrugged. "I've seen and done a lot of things that have desensitised me somewhat," he replied. "And I suppose I still resent the way everybody turned on me after I made it clear how unhappy I was that mom should take up with Josefa so soon." He paused and headed back to the vehicle. "But I'm here now and I'm going to make good on my absence."

"I hear words, Davy. But I want to see some actions."

"You will. And I don't like *Davy*. Nobody's called me that in twenty years."

"What do you prefer to be called?" she asked incredulously.

He shrugged. "My friends call me Big Dave..."

Delilah laughed as she got behind the wheel. "Well, that's just ridiculous. It's Davy, or Lomu..."

"Well, make it Lomu," he said sardonically. "And if you want action, then that's exactly what you are going to get."

"Where are we going now?" she asked as she turned the tiny 4x4 around and drove back out through the palm-lined track.

"You mentioned the consortium," he said. "That sounds like as good a start as any..."

THREE

"You wanna clean that?"

Lomu looked at his shoulder. The blood was fresh, and he slipped his hand under his shirt and checked his fingers. He knew the wound would heal but flying so soon after an injury had made the wound swell and stitches didn't tend to give. "No," he replied. "I'll have a swim later; the salt water will help."

"Old wives' tale," Delilah said incredulously. "That's what we were always told as kids, but even water this clear has parasites and pollutants."

Lomu shrugged as he got out of the vehicle. He looked around him. The development had stalled. But it would be quite a development. The footings were in for a substantial building. Lomu knew little about construction, but the graffitied sign showing an artist's rendition of the development showed six buildings, each five storeys high and linked by palm-lined walkways to a central hub that he supposed would house the restaurants, bars, spa, gymnasium and entertainment area, as well as the hotel reception. The sign showed an aerial rendition, too. The complex was to be encircled by a pool moat with swim-up bars and several smaller pools dotted about the complex.

"Shit..." Lomu commented flatly.

"This can all be returned to nature," said Delilah. "It's not too late. The ground can be bulldozed with earth and replanted."

"But not the shrine," he replied, looking at the far end of the development where the ground stepped up to a slope. "Once that's gone, it's gone."

"It's still there. For now."

"But this is holy ground."

"And that's the big difference," she replied. "It's folklore."

"All religion is fucking folklore!"

"Don't cuss, Davy. The family don't stand for it."

Lomu looked at her, but for some reason he felt compelled to apologise. She had reminded him of his aunt and mother. They never did stand for bad language. He shrugged and said, "Sorry..." He paused. "Habit. I have a soldier's vocabulary."

Delilah did not reply. She was watching a figure approaching them. "I think there's trouble coming..." Lomu turned and watched the man walking casually towards them. He did not have to watch for too long to see he was a sizeable figure. "That's Dan Carter. He's an Australian, one of McGregor's stooges."

"McGregor?" Lomu asked.

"I'm guessing Marie hasn't told you as much as I thought she had..." She paused, watching two more men approaching on quadbikes. "Yep, trouble for sure."

"You're trespassing!" The man called Carter shouted in a heavy Australian accent. "Turn around and get off this property!"

The two men stopped their quadbikes just in front of Carter and switched off their engines. Both men looked at the man as to what they should do next.

"I think you're the ones trespassing," Lomu said coldly. "I suggest you make the ground good and get the fuck out of town." Carter laughed and when he looked at the other two men, they joined in right on que. "This is holy ground. You know it and I know it."

Carter scoffed. "Holy ground? Some bullshit stories about sea snakes and caves and hidden underground lakes? Fijian mythology at its best, yet without the imagination of other more advanced cultures. Well, apart from the fucking *Abbo's*, that is. Jesus Christ, if you want to know about the worst story tellers on earth, then look no further than the fucking Aborigines of Australia!"

Lomu walked towards the Australian and the other two men immediately squared up. "Virgin birth, making a blind man see, resurrection? That's just a few stories in a book full of bullshit called the Bible. Don't you dare stand on sacred Fijian soil and ridicule our culture and heritage..." He cast a hand slowly over the development. "But I see you've already done that..."

"We have the planning permission and building permits in place."

"That's a lie!" Delilah snapped. "The development is paused because of new evidence!"

Carter laughed. He had a rugged, sunburnt complexion, but it did not hide the bruising around his left eye. A greenish yellow with flecks of purple. He looked the type to play rough, and there were a host of tiny scars around his lips that indicated he had been in a few fights over the years. "Because a boy said he had found a religious artifact? Where's the proof? The authorities have granted you an extension period. The clock is ticking *sweetie pie*. I understand the young man had an accident..."

"He was murdered!" Delilah retorted.

"Unfortunate. I gather there are no suspects, and the police have no further leads," Carter replied, unperturbed. "Misadventure is how the coroner is going to rule cause of death..."

"We'll get the evidence we need," Delilah said icily.

"Bad timing. For you, that is." Carter paused. "The authorities will have us back in work within a few days. You see, there's an election coming, and we will not only be providing work to get the project built, but we will be employing over three hundred locals and a dozen or more foreign workers in management positions who will be spending their money locally. Now, how much money do you think that will put into the economy?" He grinned. "And with two thousand extra tourists a week spending their hard-earned money on the island, how thorough do you think the government will want the local police to investigate?"

Lomu walked closer. There was now only a few metres between him and the two other men. "You're not the boss," he said. "I can tell a lackie when I see one. You're all shirt and trousers and fuck-all in the middle. You think you're the shit, but you're just somebody else's shit. Where is your boss?"

Without warning, one of the men lunged forwards and swung an ill-planned punch and missed, but kindly presented his chin to Lomu's right fist. It was a lightning reaction, and neither of the men left standing would have imagined it working out that way, but it did. The man was poleaxed and the only sound louder than the impact of

Lomu's ham-sized fist smashing bone was the sound of him landing on the earth and the air escaping his lungs.

"That's assault!" Carter shouted when he regained some composure.

"That was self-defence," Lomu replied, apparently untroubled by the incident. "Assault will be what happens next if you don't walk away."

Behind Carter two more quadbikes and a pickup truck bounced on the rough ground and headed towards them. The Australian smiled. "The key to life is to hold all the cards." He paused. "Dead boys, missing girls. The last thing this community needs is more in the way of bad luck..."

Delilah was about to jump in, but Lomu held up his hand and said to Carter, "I reckon you've got something to say. So, how about you stop pissing about and say it?"

"No. I think we're done here." Carter looked at the man next to him and nodded towards the man on the ground. "For fuck's sake, get him onto his side and check his airway!" He looked back at Lomu and said, "There were rumours that the prodigal son was set to return. Do everyone you care for a favour. Tell them to accept the money we're paying them to pack up their meagre belongings and get on with their lives. This development is going to happen, whatever the human price..."

FOUR

Delilah drove them to Lomu's family home. It did not take long because the far boundary of the development backed onto their plot. Lomu appeared tense. It was right about now that he realised just how long twenty years was in the grand scheme of things, and maybe he should not have bothered. But there was a part of him that was glad he had, despite how difficult the next few hours would probably prove to be.

Carter had left on one of the quadbikes and the unconscious man had been loaded rather unceremoniously into the bed of the pickup truck. Nothing had escalated, and Lomu was glad it hadn't. There had been seven pairs of hands and feet to get through, and even if he managed to take on such overwhelming odds and survive, there were simply too many variables – too many chances of a lucky punch or a sneaky knife. He had noticed that Carter carried a sheath knife on his right hip and suspected that he would not have hesitated in using it. But it had not come to that. Lomu and Delilah had been left alone and she had driven them back out of the development and down the seven-hundred metres of coastal track to the Lomu – and he supposed, now the Mani family homestead.

The sea like so much of Fiji's main island was calm. The outer reefs created the surf as the swells peaked in shallow water, and once they had broken into white water, the deeper water of the lagoons dissipated the swell leaving many of the beaches with just a gentle shore break rather than surfable waves. There were notable exceptions, but here the surf never got over three feet high, which made it perfect for fleet fishing in small boats and canoes that were hauled up the beach overnight. Lomu watched some children playing in the tiny waves. Thirty years ago, it could have been him and his friends in those wonderfully giddy childhood days when the future wasn't even a thought considered and the past was merely yesterday and the care-free fun that was had, and the laughter brought on by thoughts of the day before.

"Takes you back, doesn't it?"

Lomu would have to agree. He watched chickens pecking where the short grass met the sand, torn between the larger land-dwelling grubs and insects, and the tiny sand fleas on the beach. On the hottest days he remembered they would herd the pigs into the sea to cool off and wash away ticks. He imagined the tourists would enjoy watching swimming pigs through the flipped lens of their selfies, but knew it wasn't going to happen. There was no way that the Lomus, or he supposed the Manis, could coexist next door to two-thousand tourists, and all that would bring. It was more than the uncomfortable proximity to tourism. The impact on their way of life would be unmanageable. Jet skis and speedboats would hinder fishing, swimmers and snorkellers would damage the seabed and destroy the habitat for fish, thus affecting their sustainable food source.

The homestead would become an attraction as wealthy tourists gawped at the traditional Fijian way of life or farming and fishing on a family and pin-money scale.

"You don't live here?"

Delilah shook her head. "No, I have an apartment in Suva that goes with my job there. That gives me the ability to save for a place of my own."

"You don't want to continue the way of the families living here?"

She shook her head as she parked the open-topped Suzuki under a lean-to with a palm frond roof. She switched off the engine and settled back in the seat as she watched the children playing in the water. "I respect the family's desire to retain the old ways, but sadly, the writing is on the wall. The McGregor Enterprises development aside, our way of life is for the history books. You know that. Which was why you bailed out for a different life when you were just sixteen."

"It wasn't just that..."

"Come off it! The cities and shops, the different countries..."

"The bullets, the bodies, the twenty-mile marches, the shitting in the woods..."

She laughed. "OK, but what you found on the other side of the world was obviously enough to keep you there." She paused. "Why else would you stay away for so long?"

Lomu didn't reply. He knew that it had been down to sadness for the loss of his father, anger at his mother for moving on so quickly with his father's best friend, hurt pride, stubbornness and ego. It had been with a heady mix of emotions that he had boarded the recruitment ship. He wondered whether the recruitment ships would be subject to similar investigations in years to come as *Windrush* had.

Perhaps. However, recruitment to the British Army was still a large part of Fijian culture – in much the same spirit as the Gurkhas recruited from Nepal - and the ships might not come in unannounced as they had in Lomu's day, but Fijians plugged the gaps in the British armed forces along with several Caribbean countries and Ghana making up the highest number of recruits. It wasn't just the Gurkhas who now had the tradition of proudly serving in the British Army.

Lomu looked up as an attractive woman in her early thirties stepped out of a long hut made from wood with a straw roof. The hut or house – one of a dozen on the homestead – was a traditional Fijian design called a bure, and there were some made from stone as well, but all were a single-storey design and shared a common straw roof. Beside some were upturned canoes and surfboards, old motorcycles in various condition or states of repair and a few pickup trucks. Lomu remembered that there was never much money growing up, but everybody had seemed happy. A toddler padded out from the hut and trotted to the woman, who swept him up in her arms and walked towards them, beaming a smile as she approached.

"I can't believe you actually came," she said. "I thought that Delilah would come by and report a no show..." She put the toddler down and stepped in to hug her brother.

Lomu hugged her, lifting her off the ground enough for her toes to drag in the dirt. "I'm sorry it's been so long, Marie..."

She pulled away and slapped him hard across the face. "You should have come back!" she yelled at him, catching him completely unaware. "I had to deal with so much after you left. I lost *my* dad, too. But more than that, I lost *you* as well..."

"This is going well..." Lomu cupped his cheek and turned around to see a tall, elegant and beautiful girl in her teens. "I'm Kalara," she said in the off-handed manner that teens managed so effortlessly. "I didn't *lose* anyone, but it would have been nice to meet my uncle before I was thirteen..."

Marie looked at him expectantly, then shrugged. "Kalara is my oldest. My husband, Jake is working away. He's on oil rigs in the Indian Ocean. He doesn't get back much," she looked sadly at her daughter and Delilah. "But my girls help out, I don't know what I'd do without them. We're the sisterhood!" She smiled and patted the toddler on the head and added, "Yami was what we would call a surprise baby. But a wonderful surprise. I was only nineteen when I had Kalara, and I vowed I was done after that..."

"That?" Kalara feigned mock protest. "Only because you thought you had created perfection, so there was little hope for another." She smiled as she walked over and swept her brother off his feet. "Ah, but he's gorgeous, despite his competition!"

Lomu smiled at his niece and nephew, if he had been stubborn enough not to regret his staying away before now, he was certainly changing his mind as he saw the family likeness in the two children. Marie reached a hand to his shoulder and said, "Get over the slap, you big idiot. It had to be done. Now, I've got tea, coffee or Milo..."

"Milo!" Lomu said a little too excitedly, feeling like a child for the first time in twenty years. "I haven't had that since... well, before..."

"One of the better things Australia have given us," Delilah said of the chocolate malt drink that came in powder form in a tin.

"Yeah, I'll take Vegemite and Milo, but we can live

without tourist developments like that..." Marie thumbed over her shoulder at the mounds of earth on the edge of the homestead that had been cleared from the site. "You've met them, by all accounts."

"News travels fast," Lomu replied, following her towards the hut.

"I know somebody working there," Marie replied.

"We all do," said Delilah. "To be fair, until the site was temporarily shut down, there were a couple of hundred locals doing casual labour on the site. That's what makes this so difficult, people are earning money from it, but if it's completed, we lose our entire way of life."

"Says big city woman with her fancy apartment and company car..." Kalara commented acidly.

"Don't sass me again, cuz..." Delilah flashed her a glare that said the teen was out of her depth or getting there real quick. "You need to get through your exams and get into college. You need to embrace modern life." She paused. "But developments like this one, that's another matter entirely."

"It's all about balance, honey," Marie told her daughter. "Never take more than you need, never ask for more than can be given and give all you can spare to help others. When we fish, we catch enough to feed us and to make a little money. We don't overfish the ocean. We don't dredge the bottom. If you need wood, then cut what you need and leave other trees to grow."

"But you like the old ways," Kalara protested.

"Because I have found what works for me, and what it has given you and your brother in their childhood. But I still like my cell phone and the internet, and I like your father to take me to a restaurant occasionally. But how we live is *our* choice, and not for developers to wipe out entirely while they destroy the environment."

The teenager remained silent. With teenagers it could have gone both ways. Vehemently keep pushing their point to the point of exasperation on their parent's part or read the situation and keep quiet for another day – on both counts convinced that they were right. Lomu had no experience of teenagers, but he had plenty of experience at not being able to get his point across to officers, and he figured it was the same thing. He patted the girl on her shoulder as they entered the bure and was instantly taken back to his childhood. They walked into an open-plan kitchen and living room, with curtains sealing off various sleeping areas. The furniture was rattan with cushions and in the corner of the living area was the smallest television set he had seen in years, and rather than flat screen, it was as deep as it was wide with a set rabbit ear antennae on top. The cynical trait in him wondered whether Marie enjoyed the old ways because she was financially incapable of enjoying modern life to the full. But then his conscience took over. Fiji was a tough place to make it if you had one foot in the past, and her talk of her children's childhood had seemed heart-felt and besides, what did modern trappings really offer over basic happiness. He would always remember his fishing trips with his father and Josefa, and he would always long for those family feasts where a whole pig had been roasted and freshly baked breads accompanied the fruits and vegetables the woman folk had prepared while the men had gathered round and manned the firepit and prodded both flame and ember and meat with sharpened implements and sticks, while the younger children hung around for crispy crackling treats that were lovingly tossed their way while they waited for the thicker cuts of pork to cook through.

The memory of that alone was worth a TV streaming service, a thousand drive-thru meals and a hundred fancy restaurants.

Marie made coffee for them all, and a large cup of Milo for Lomu. He found an iPhone cable hanging from a socket and put his phone on to charge while he sipped the hot, malty chocolate drink and was taken instantly back to his childhood. His mother would occasionally allow it to cool and serve it with a scoop of her own homemade coconut ice cream as a floater.

"Where is mom?" he asked.

"Hospital," Marie answered.

"Is she alright?"

"*She* is." Marie paused. "Josefa has cancer. He's been having chemotherapy. This will be his third round."

"What type of cancer?"

"Does it matter? Cancer is cancer."

Lomu shrugged. "I suppose..."

"Quit pretending like you care," Kalara said acidly.

"Kalara!" Marie chastened her.

"No, she's right to say it," said Lomu. "I guess I don't. One way or another."

"Really? After all this time?" Marie asked incredulously.

Lomu didn't answer, because he couldn't. He had loved the man once, like an uncle. More so, even. Like another father. The fact that the man had taken up with his mother before his father's body was even cold was something that he could not forgive. In reality, it had been a few weeks, but he remembered how he had felt, and he still felt the same way twenty-years later. Over the months that had followed, family members had argued that his mother and Josefa had always been friends and that Josefa had helped her through the most awful of times. Disbelief, uncertainty, fear and the constant need for normality are all parts of the process of grieving, and who was anyone to say what was best for his mother? Certainly not a sixteen-year-old boy with virtually no life experience.

"I guess you really hold a grudge," Delilah commented.

Lomu shrugged. "I'm here to help you find a missing girl," he said.

"Her name is Monique," Marie said sharply. "And she's *your* half-sister. And I'll remind you that she's *all* of mom's daughter. So, she loves her just like you and just like me."

"I doubt mom loves us the same..."

"Idiot!" Marie snapped. "You're her first born, her son! If anything, she probably has a special place for you! Get over yourself and realise that not only is her daughter missing, but her husband has cancer, and you know what? It's not going well for Josefa. And before you even think about carrying on with this stupid twenty-year sulk, she has been with Josefa longer than she was ever with pappa, and if you had been around even just once every few years, you would realise that they have a happy marriage."

"They're married?"

"Of course."

"Why didn't I know that?"

Marie rolled her eyes and put down her coffee. "Try writing, try visiting. Anyway, it was felt you might try to ruin the day, so I was told not to tell you."

"Josefa said that?" Lomu replied gruffly.

"No. Mom said that. Josefa wanted you to come and try to make amends."

"Oh," he replied lamely. He turned and looked out of the window. There was only fifty metres of short grass to the beach and the sea glistened in the afternoon sun. It looked inviting and as he watched the gentle waves lap the shore, he was reminded of the wound to his shoulder and side. Despite what Delilah had said of parasites and pollution, he knew the crystal-clear water would soothe the swelling and tenderness and go a long way towards cleaning it. "I need a swim," he said.

"A swim?" Kalara asked incredulously.

Lomu shrugged. "Give me an hour and then we'll work out a plan of action." He left them standing in the kitchen, but he knew that the swim was more about focusing his mind and taking on board what he had been told. Swimming had always calmed him and allowed him to focus, and he could not think of a better place to swim than in front of his childhood home.

FIVE

The water was slightly colder than the air temperature and Lomu felt the coolness rush over him as he dived over the small breaker and swam close to the seabed. The salinity was high, and it not only stung his eyes, but the wound at his shoulder and he knew at once that the sea would help rather than hinder. He barely felt the bullet wound at his ribs which would suggest he was healing well.

He breached the surface and swam the next hundred metres in a slow, confident crawl, settling into his breathing and inhaling on every third stroke, which allowed him to breath under each arm. He remembered Josefa had corrected him as a child, when he only ever inhaled on his right. If you could breathe equally as well on each side, then you never struggled when the ocean saw fit to push swells laterally towards you.

Lomu stopped stroking and rolled onto his back and floated for a while. He wasn't overly concerned about predators. The larger sharks usually remained on the outer reefs, or in deep water where the makos and tiger sharks tended to dwell. As a child, he and his friends had called in shark pups to the shore by slapping the water and feeding them with scraps of fish and meat left over from dinner. They had named them individually and knew from the size and markings which shark was which. Sometimes larger sharks had cruised the shore and come into the shallows, but he never remembered anybody getting bitten, and they often walked knee-deep amongst them. Lomu had recalled the sharks taking turns for the scraps. To Fijian children, they were like dogs. He wondered whether the practice had been continued or discouraged. He couldn't imagine Fiji had ducked the health and safety mentality, nor that the practice could have continued if it meant tourists might see it for free, when they could otherwise sign up for day-long catered boat trips and shark feeding experiences as part of expensive concession packages. He soon snapped out of his thoughts as he was bitten by several sea lice. Each bite felt like a wasp sting, and he snatched a breath, dived down and grabbed handfuls of sand and rubbed it all over him. He then pushed off the bottom and swam hard for the surface, where he launched into a fast crawl. He was no longer getting bitten, and even though the sea lice bites had been painful, the pain did not linger. He settled his stroke down, reminded that the ocean around Fiji harboured many creatures you would not find in the Med, and smooth strokes tended not to attract predators in the way that erratic strokes and splashing did. He was soon reminded of this as he saw the banded sea snake rising to investigate who was splashing so wildly in its lagoon. Thirty times more venomous than a king cobra, bites were thankfully rare because of its small mouth and teeth set far back in its jaw. But he had known fishermen die from bites on their fingers as they had sorted the catch from their nets, so he changed direction and kept on stroking and kicking until he was confident that he was clear, then he changed direction and headed for the shore.

Lomu stood when his fingers clawed at the sand, and he waded the last few metres to the beach. The salt had soothed his wounds, and he supposed the seawater had gone a long way to make his feet smell better, too.

There were three men waiting for him. All three were native Fijians of predominantly African heritage. Just like Lomu. However, they were all six inches shorter and several stone lighter. They stood stock-still and looked to have bad intentions on their minds.

"You are to leave Fiji," said the man in the middle. "Right now."

"I'm going to leave," Lomu replied. "But when I'm good and ready."

"Just go," another chipped in.

Lomu looked expectantly at the third man. "You want to add to this?"

The man stared at him and said, "We don't want no trouble, *mon*."

"Too late for that."

The first man to have spoken said, "On the next flight."

Lomu smiled. "OK, so I guess we have ourselves a problem. Now fellas, I know that you are speaking for somebody else. I also know that you're all three wondering whether the money or incentive you have been given to send me this message is going to be worth it." He paused. "Let me tell you; it's not. Now, the smart play would be to concede that you've delivered the message and to walk away. Because I'm not leaving, and I won't be pushed into leaving either." The men glanced at one another, then looked back at Lomu. "Decision time," he added, taking a step closer to them. "Or do I send a message back to your employer?" He paused. "One message or three, it makes no odds to me."

"You don't know what you're dealing with," said the man in the middle. Lomu took him to be the leader. "This development is going ahead. Your family should get used to the idea and quit stalling."

"A boy was killed."

"Not on my employer's property." The man paused. "And a temporary stoppage has been called while the authorities investigate claims of damage to private property. The boy's death has nothing to do with our employer."

"You'd better be certain of that, or you could pay the price, too." Lomu looked hard at the man and said, "I believe your company has damaged the steps to a shrine, and that shrine is nobody's property. It is a religious and historical artifact."

"Mumbo-jumbo, *mon,*" the man replied.

"Your heritage isn't mumbo-jumbo," Lomu corrected him.

"I don't care about anything other than my pay cheque. Like many of the men here, we need the development to feed our families." He paused. "So, listen when I say you should leave..."

Lomu stepped closer still. "You're in my way," he said.

"There's plenty of room on the beach," one of the book-ends pointed out.

"But I want to go that way..." He stepped closer. Just a pace between them now. "And you're still in my way."

Never back down, never apologise.

One of the bookends moved, but the other two stood still. He would have to give them credit, they were doing the job they had been paid for. Lomu caught sight of someone high above them, several hundred feet into the development. So, he was being watched. And so were the lackies. They were not going to back down if their line manager was checking on their work.

Lomu nodded. So, that was how it was going to play out. Enough talk. It was time for a demonstration. He turned without further word and walked away.

"Where are you going?" the leader barked at him.

Lomu said nothing and continued across the sand. He did not see, but could imagine them standing there, flummoxed. They had been given an order and now they could not carry it out. When all the words were said and done, they had been here for one reason and one reason only. They were basic people and basic people never thought outside the box. They had been paid to cause trouble and now trouble was walking away. Lomu heard the shift of sand, caught sight of the shadow in the late afternoon sun. He would have bet on one of the bookends, but it didn't matter. He dropped his left knee, shifting his height by around two feet, twisted a half turn and powered out a side kick which connected with the man's own kneecap. There was just enough time to hear the bone splintering, the ligaments snapping like thick elastic bands, before his screams drowned everything else out. Lomu watched the other two men, now frozen to the spot. They had been slightly behind the man as he had charged forwards, but with him writhing on the sand, indecision had halted them a fraction too long. Lomu smashed his fist into the nearest man's throat, snapping back his head and causing him to rasp for breath. The man fell onto his backside, both hands clasping his throat as he struggled to breathe. Lomu watched the man manipulate his own squashed airway to inhale precious air, and with that standing between life and death, he was out of the fight and not looking to get back into it anytime soon. That just left the man who had done the talking. Only he wasn't talking now. Now, he was holding a knife. The blade was long and thin and wickedly sharp. Lomu had seen the type before. Its curved blade and wooden handle gave a distinctive look, and it was a popular choice with fishermen the world over who used it for a variety of tasks including filleting fish.

"You have a choice," said Lomu, now ignoring the knife and staring the man in his eyes. "Toss the knife and walk away or come at me with everything you've got."

"Doesn't seem like much of a choice," the man replied, stepping over his friend with the breathing problem and separating the distance between himself and Lomu to two paces at best.

"No. But I guarantee if you come at me with that, I'll kill you."

"You like to talk."

Lomu shrugged. "I've warned you, so it's your choice. But I promise I'll take your life right here on the sand."

"It's not going to come to that..."

Lomu looked up at the sound of the Australian twang and saw Carter standing on the edge of the development. He was high above them, standing proudly on a mound of soil and rubble with a pistol in his hand. The pistol was aiming at Lomu, who was already weighing up his odds if he sprinted and zig-zagged back across the beach to the village. Most gunfights - or what Lomu knew as CQB (close quarters battles) – with a pistol took place at distances of ten feet or less and had a seventy percent hit rate. At twenty feet it was more like twenty percent. But figures were one thing and Lomu had consistently put bullets in bullseyes at one-hundred metres with a 9mm Browning, and if he wasn't mistaken, Carter had one in his hand right now. It was likely the Australian would fall into the ninety percent who would miss a moving target at twenty feet, but there was no way of knowing.

Lomu heard the laughter and the other men heard it too. A gaggle of young children ran across the sand and pulled at Lomu's shorts. The youngest looked like Marie's toddler, the oldest appeared to be no more than nine years old. The girls wore brightly coloured dresses, and the boys were simply bare-chested in shorts looking like miniature versions of Lomu. Calls to come home, that dinner was ready, that he was to come home right now – all shouted at once and amongst laughter and shrieks of excitement. Lomu looked up at Carter, but he had put the gun away and was looking on with amusement and a final sneer that told Lomu as he walked away, that they were not done yet.

SIX

"Well, I wouldn't have sent Yami over there if I knew they had guns!"

"One gun," Lomu corrected her. "That Australian fella."

"One, ten... It makes no difference! A gun is a gun. They're illegal in Fiji, anyway. That sort, at least," Marie looked at Delilah for confirmation, who nodded.

"Yes, handguns are for certain," Delilah replied. "Farmers have shotguns, and some people have permits for hunting rifles." She nodded towards the shotgun hanging on the wall, a battered and worn tool of subsistence farmers, like many in the homes in the village. "Maybe collectors have permits for handguns, but I don't think it gives them the right to carry them..."

"Well, no permit is going to give anyone permission to point it at someone," Marie chipped in. "We should call the police."

Lomu shook his head. "Not yet," he said adamantly. "I imagine this McGregor character will have the police in his pocket. A few key officers that have the ability to stall or halt a murder investigation, or at least tamper with evidence or witnesses." He paused, helping himself to some of the fried fish Marie had placed on the table. She served it with some sweet potato dip. On queue half a dozen young children burst in and grabbed a piece or two each, smeared them in the sweet potato and tucked in hungrily. Lomu snatched a couple more pieces before the plate of food was decimated. Several of the children had double-dipped and he bit into the tempura battered fish as he looked at snotty noses and messy lips, deciding to give the sweet potato dip a miss. The scene reminded him of his childhood and the communal living that sometimes became a daily occurrence. They had certainly had their favourite *bures* to head to for sweet treats or snacks, or fruit punch. Each house had a mother that outdid another, and it looked like Marie's afternoon deep-fried snacks were top of the childrens' list.

"What are you going to do first?" Marie asked.

Lomu finished his mouthful and stood up. "Are you my designated driver or is there a vehicle I can use?" he asked Delilah.

"I'm heading back to Suva to catch up on some emails and file a few things, then I'm coming back here for dinner."

"Dinner?" Lomu asked incredulously. "Damn, I didn't want any fuss..."

"The prodigal son returns..." Marie said acidly.

"Jesus... Don't bother..." Lomu shrugged. "Is that how I'm seen by everyone? A wasteful squanderer who returns and all is forgiven?" He paused. "I don't ask for anything and expect nothing in return. *You're* the one who begged me to come out here and help you..."

"I'm sorry," she replied coolly. "It's just that while *you* left and travelled the world, *I* stayed behind. I dealt with all the family problems over the years, and now you come back, and mom asked us all to prepare a feast and celebrate your return..."

"Well, don't bother on my account," he replied and headed out through the door. Delilah had already caught him up as he set out across the dry earth towards the Suzuki SUV. "Take me back to the city," he said. "I'll hire a vehicle and get started. The sooner I find the girl, the sooner I'll be out of here."

"Your half-sister," she corrected him. "And her name is Monique."

"Fine."

"And what makes you so sure you'll find her?" Delilah slipped behind the steering wheel of the Suzuki and started the engine. She waited until Lomu dropped heavily into the passenger seat, the vehicle bouncing on its springs. "She's most likely to have been killed by the same people who murdered Mustafa."

"Then why the certainty from everybody else that she's still alive?"

"I guess they can't accept it," she replied as they bounced across the rough ground in front of the development. "That's how it is with loved ones, isn't it? Even after they're dead and you've seen the body, sometimes you simply can't believe it's true."

Lomu nodded. He had been surrounded by death during his years in the army, and especially during his tours of Afghanistan, and later as a bodyguard and mercenary in the usual places – Central Africa, Iraq, Syria and a few of the Balkan countries. Some deaths he had accepted straight away, but there were friends and colleagues that he still had trouble letting go of. "Where is Mustafa's body?" he asked.

"At the mortuary," she replied. "The coroner hasn't yet

released his body because the family are struggling to come up with a funeral plan..."

"He's on ice until they have the readies?"

"Readies?"

"Money."

"Yes," she nodded. "That's my thinking."

"Isn't he from a Muslim family?" Lomu asked, then added, "They've got to get their loved ones in the ground pretty damned quick. Inside twenty-four hours, usually."

She shook her head. "Diluted, I suppose. They have Muslim names, just as we have a mix of Christian and Polynesian names. Look at Josefa, he sounds like a Muslim, but he's not one to shy away from a roasted pig."

Lomu nodded. The mention of Josefa made him tense. The man had been such a large part of his childhood, that he simply couldn't move past the perceived betrayal. Although the uncomfortable truth nagged at him that the man had been with his mother longer than his own father had, and now that he learned Josefa had cancer, he couldn't help thinking his hatred and indifference seemed trite. And yet, he still could not find it in himself to let it go. He took a deep breath to calm his emotion. It didn't work. He looked up at the mountain, realising that they were heading back to the capital on a different road. Delilah had shown him where Mustafa had died and had taken a diversion to do so.

"What was he doing up there?" Lomu asked, nodding towards the mountain.

"Monique and Mustafa got it into their heads that they could find proof of the existence of Degei, or at least conclusive evidence that Kintoto stands on sacred and historical ground."

"Really?" he replied. He knew that the shrine was seen as sacred, but he never really put much stock in it. Just simple tribal belief, which his family still honoured today. It sounded as though the two teenagers had got more caught up in their family's cause than they should have. Beyond the realm of good sense, anyway.

"Well, superstition and religion are all founded on fact. So, the facts may become distorted over time and the retelling. Look at the King James Bible. Most of it was penned by monks in the seventeenth century. Likewise, look at most depictions of Jesus and the Disciples. They're white, many have red hair. Jesus would have been as dark as your average Palestinian or Egyptian. But in the Holy Land, there is no doubt that he existed, it's just the stories and depictions that have changed over time."

"So, Fiji really did have a sea serpent as a god?" Lomu smiled.

"Doubtful, I'll admit," Delilah said with a shrug. "But before influences from India, and before the islands were populated with African slaves brought over by the British to harvest sugarcane, religion was practised in sacred locations by our Polynesian ancestors and many of the stories that were written had the common bond that features in all religions. That is the moral standards condemning such things as murder, theft and adultery, and that sacrificing wants for giving something to those less fortunate are qualities that will allow you safe passage into the afterlife." She paused. "No matter where you are in the world, religion guides virtue."

"That's because Kings and Emperors wanted a subservient, law-abiding populace."

"No doubt. But *people* decided how to behave in society. Otherwise, the majority would take what they want and give nothing back. Whatever the religion, and whyever it started, all religions teach the same lessons in how to behave towards others. Whether it's God and *His* prophets through Christianity, Judaism and Islam, or Buddha and Hinduism or Sikhism, or the sun gods of South America or sea serpents of Oceania, many of the expectations are the same."

Lomu nodded but said nothing else on the subject as he watched the sun glisten off the ocean and the various water sports going on in the bay. He tried to remember the last time he had been to a similar climate and figured it would have to have been Belize with the British army. He had completed his jungle training in Borneo with the SAS but there had been no downtime. In Belize, he had ended the training with a week's R&R and gone diving, parasailing and wakeboarding with the lads. Even scuba-dived on the world's second largest reef. He recalled that he had felt homesick there for the first time in years, the water so similar to his native Fiji.

Delilah dropped him at the Hertz office, and he rented a Jeep Compass. He had used his MI5 black Visa card. Part of him wondering whether he would ever return to the Security Service. He was technically AWOL. He smiled as he typed in the pin, picturing Neil Ramsay turning purple and going apoplectic when he would be met with the query from accounts and forced to justify what an agent was doing in Fiji. MI5 and MI6 used what they called officers to carry out their work. These officers were backed up by agents, usually people they turned within terrorism organisations and crime rings, or occasionally within the military or governments of foreign powers. Lomu was classed as an agent because the unit he worked with operated outside of MI5's parameters, even though they were now employed as 'consultants' answerable only to Neil Ramsay, who was classed as their Liaison Officer, and Simon Mereweather, who was the Director General of the Security Service. Lomu had been recruited by one of these 'consultants', a former SAS Captain named Rashid, who along with other mercenaries had been used in a deniable operation. Lomu had proved himself an invaluable asset and had later joined the unit. Only now, he was wondering whether he should stop playing with fire before he got seriously burnt. He had taken two bullets – fortunately low powered .22 subsonic rounds - on his last operation and as he had watched the glistening ocean, the white sand beaches and the people enjoying both, he found himself questioning the fragility of life and the wisdom in tempting fate. He had completed three tours of Afghanistan with too numerous enemy contacts to put a figure on, gone up against terrorists in a dozen operations with the SAS and to his reckoning, gone into battle more than twenty times on the mercenary circuit. His work with MI5 had seen him often cobbling together a plan and relying on luck as he followed a man named King, to his mind, one of the best, toughest, (and luckiest) operatives who ever lived. And even *his* luck was going to change one day.

The Jeep was underwhelming. Lomu had imagined it would have a lumpy, torquey engine and be twice the size, but what he got was an American version of the Suzuki and suspected the closest place the Jeep had been to America was past a *McDonalds* restaurant on the back of a vehicle transporter in Delhi. It certainly had the feel of a car put together in India or Asia.

The Colonial War Memorial Hospital looked exactly as it sounded. Similar in design to the metropolitan and government buildings of the Caribbean or that of an American tobacco plantation in the Deep South, the colonial design with covered walkway balconies with balustrades, and whitewashed exterior belied the fact it was Fiji's largest and oldest hospital that served as headquarters for the island's nursing college and its only morgue. It also boasted the island's largest emergency room and most advanced surgery. Palm trees lined the short grass lawn and smaller palms ran along the edge of the various pathways. Lomu found what he wanted at the rear of the building. As a rule, the emergency room was at the front of most hospitals with the most parking, and the mortuary was at the rear. Simple logistics and priorities. The reception was always on a gable end, usually the closest to the entrance.

The mortuary doors were closed, but there was an orderly smoking and texting on his phone, his white scrubs looking well-used and stained. He looked up as Lomu approached.

"I'm looking for a man who can make things happen."

The orderly frowned. "What up, *mon*?"

"Doors opening, no questions." He paused, unsure how to continue knowing how vulgar he was about to sound. "Three hundred dollars."

The man dropped his cigarette on the ground and stubbed it out with his foot. He was already putting his phone back in his pocket. Three hundred Fijian dollars was just over a hundred pounds, but it was three weeks' wages for the orderly, and they both knew it. "Come with me..."

"I need to see my cousin," Lomu lied. "Fifteen-year-old boy, named Mustafa."

"The boy killed on top of Nakandua?"

"Yes."

"Wow, sorry *mon*..." The orderly checked his watch as he opened a side door and stepped inside. Lomu noted that the door was extra wide to accommodate trolleys and gurneys. "The police got no answers, but no surprise there..."

Lomu frowned. "How do you figure?"

The man shrugged. He glanced down the corridor, then guided Lomu through another door. "Word is the boy was looking for something that would halt the development at Kintoto Point. That's sacred ground out there, even if local administration wants to turn a blind eye. Money talks. Still, great job opportunities with plenty of tips, and sure as shit beats this gig..." They reached the end of a short corridor painted in cream and scuffed so deeply that the plaster had been gouged. Decades of paint patching had covered the scuffs and added inches of thickness so that the wall was proud of the skirting below. "Boy must have found it," the man observed. "Otherwise, why else would he have been killed?"

Lomu said nothing. He had the uneasy feeling that he was up against an irresistible force. The belief that someone working for the development company had killed Mustafa and were responsible for Monique's disappearance had been voiced publicly, and yet nothing had stuck. The police had called off the search for Monique and had got nowhere with the investigation into Mustafa's death. A clemency had been granted in that there was now a deadline for any forthcoming evidence that Kintoto Point was indeed sacred ground in accordance with Fijian faith and mythology. After that date, which Delilah had told him was now less than one week away, then the development would restart under a new compliance order, that could not be overturned a second time and Lomu's family, and at least a half dozen other families would be essentially homeless, and hundreds of years of settlement would be bulldozed to make way for swim-up lodges and water sports hire.

"Need to see the green..." the man said, hovering in front of the next closed door. He looked at Lomu and said, "I will leave you alone for ten minutes. Don't touch the damned body, and don't leave any of your DNA on it... I mean, kissing the boy goodbye on his forehead will leave your DNA, so don't be tempted..." He paused, watching as Lomu counted out the three-hundred dollars. "Not that you will be, I hear the boy was a mess..." He glanced up at Lomu, fearing he had overstepped the mark. Lomu would have sworn he could see what the man was going to spend his windfall on in his own glossy eyes. It was a look of pure greed. The money was a huge deal to him, but then again, a few weeks' undisclosed salary was a game changer for most people, and the location and exchange value was relative. All the man had to do was open a few doors and turn a blind eye. The man eagerly held out his hand and snatched the notes but felt them hold fast in Lomu's grip.

"You keep watch for me. I don't want anybody interrupting me as I pray for him."

"Hey, I got you in. I never agreed to babysit you, *mon...*"

"Another hundred when you escort me without drama back to the rear of the hospital." That made a month's pay. The man nodded eagerly. "Where's the coroner?"

The man checked his watch. "He no here now. Back in a couple of hours, ready for the nightshift. Golf course, maybe. Anyone unfortunate enough to kick the bucket is held in the cool room until the night shift come on to process, or file paperwork left over from the day shift." The man paused and smiled. "The place is as quiet as a morgue..."

SEVEN

Lomu had insisted that the man show him through. He had found the relevant refrigerated locker from the wall-mounted chart. Mustafa's surname had been Hussein. The boy's body was in the second locker to the right, the third high. One of twelve lockers occupied in a bank of sixteen. By the time Lomu had found a pair of latex gloves and opened the drawer, the man had returned to the door and was looking furtively down the corridor. Only dull security lighting lined the corridor walls, the main lights being motion activated to save electricity. Now the corridor took on a dull, eerie hue exacerbated by the pale, cream walls.

Lomu unzipped the bag and took a breath before opening it. Mustafa's eyes were closed, his lips slightly parted to reveal a glimpse of a dried and shrunken tongue. At this stage, the body was merely a carcass and slowly, but ever constantly losing moisture. The trauma was obvious. A round indent around the diameter of a cricket ball, and a quarter of a cricket ball's volume deep. There were tiny cuts all around the indent, where the skin had split from the force of the blow. Lomu imagined the inside of the boy's head would be a mess. Bone fragments would have imploded into the brain and a bullet wouldn't have done the job any quicker. No accident. Not a chance. Ignoring the porter's instructions, he unzipped the body bag further and took out the boy's right hand. There were six stages of rigor mortis - Absent: The body is still able to get a small amount of oxygen anaerobically. The muscles are still soft and movable. Minimal: The body's muscles will start to turn stiff in this stage. The face muscles are the first to be affected. Moderate: More body muscles begin to harden, and it becomes obvious that the body is no longer loose or flexible. Advanced: Most of the muscles in the body are now stiff and do not bend. Complete: All muscles in the body become hard and inflexible. Passed: Rigor mortis is complete, and the body now relaxes and moves into the phases of livor mortis and finally decomposition.

The boy's hand felt soft, cold and malleable, as it would be after so many days. Lomu turned the hand over. There was bruising on the knuckles and scratches around his wrist. He checked the boy's left hand. Just scratches. Someone had tried to restrain him, but the bruising would indicate that he had not gone down without a fight. Lomu thought about what Carter had said about a likely verdict of misadventure. Either McGregor had the coroner in his pocket, or the police. But Lomu feared it was both. A whitewash was happening, and he was damned if he knew what he could do about it. And then he remembered the bruising around Carter's left eye. Just the place a righthanded punch would land around ninety percent of the time.

Lomu looked at the trauma injury once more. It was a curious indentation, one that could never have been made by a cricket ball, no matter how fast the bowler. He imagined a baseball pitch, the ball curving in towards the poor boy's head. But it still would not have been enough force. The ball would have bounced off. It could well have fractured the skull, but not to this extent. This was something else entirely.

Voices penetrated the silence, and Lomu hurriedly replaced the boy's hand, zipped up the body bag and slid the drawer back into the refrigerated locker unit. He started out towards the door, taking off the gloves and slipping them into his pocket when the door on the opposite side of the room opened.

"Who the hell are you?" a man's voice challenged him.

Lomu turned around, feigning a look of ignorance coupled with surprise. "Sorry, I'm looking for the coroner..."

"That's me. Joseph Hu. What do you want?"

Lomu beamed a smile of brilliant white teeth. In his line of work he had been proud to have kept them all intact. "Dave Lomu. My family know Mustafa Hussein. The boy who..."

"Was killed on the mountain," Hu finished his sentence for him. "What concern is this of yours? I must say, I feel I should call security..."

"I hear that the family are struggling to pay for the funeral." He paused. "I want to help."

Joseph Hu frowned. "Strange. That sort of gesture can often be construed as an ease of conscience."

"Then I guess I'll get the money back from someone whose conscience isn't as clear as my own." He studied the man in front of him. Five feet eight, lithely built. Full of nervous energy. But surely a coroner should have a cool temperament? Lomu figured that the talk of conscience was a deflection. "How's *your* conscience, Doc?"

"What do you mean?" Hu replied quickly.

"Exactly what I say. A verdict of misadventure, that's what I'm hearing."

"And who *are* you, exactly?" He walked to his desk and picked up his phone, dialling just one number. "Hello, security? Yes, I need somebody in the mortuary," he said, all the while looking into Lomu's deep, dark eyes.

"That's a mistake," said Lomu.

"And why would that be?" Hu asked as he put down the phone.

Lomu shrugged. "Because I haven't finished with you yet."

"Are you intimidating me?"

"I don't know, am I?"

"You're one of those from the point, aren't you?"

"One of *those?*"

"One of the old tribes. Resisting the development," he said callously. "Just as you've all resisted progress, technology and society. A bunch of peasant farmers and fishermen who still hunt with spears and lament the old ways while irrefutably resisting the new." He sneered. "Wearing loin cloths while using an iPhone..."

Lomu bristled, but before he could retort the door opened, and a security officer walked in. He was quick to access the threat and he looked at the coroner, then up at Lomu, then back at the coroner. Lomu wasn't sure what the security officer's stance was, but he figured that the man's minimum wage certainly did not look worth the sacrifice.

"Well, get him out of here!" Hu shouted at the hesitant guard.

"Go get a juice and come back in ten," Lomu suggested. "I'm not going to hurt him..." he said, taking a step towards the guard. Six-feet-four and eighteen stone of bad luck and trouble for anyone foolish enough to stand in his way. "Go on, sunshine, get the fuck out of here..." Lomu watched the guard go and the door hush closed. He figured he would have five minutes, but more likely three. Three minutes for the guard to get some colleagues and come back to save his job, and more than a little face. He looked at Hu and said, "You're in somebody's pocket, aren't you? Now, what I'm going to find out is whose, and how deep those pockets go. And then I'm going to go about setting things right, and if you're someone I'm going to have to cross paths with again, then you've been warned. I'm going to get the job done, and your department are going to get busy real quick."

Hu watched as Lomu walked to the locker and pulled out the drawer containing Mustafa Hussein. He unzipped the body bag, and Hu rushed over, only for Lomu to grab him by the back of his neck. The man's fingers dug in deeply and Lomu half pulled, half lifted the man off the floor and pressed his face up against Mustafa's bloodied cheek.

"Take a look!"

"Stop it...!" Hu pleaded.

Lomu ignored him and pressed until the man's right eye was mere inches from the indentation. He pulled out the boy's hand and jammed the limp fist up against the coroner's face. "See that? Bruising! He punched his assailant. His other hand has lesions from where he was restrained! I bet he's got his assailant's skin under his fingernails! Want me to go on?" He pulled Hu back to his feet and Mustafa's arm flopped loosely off the gurney. "This boy was murdered. Now, either you are being bribed, or the police are, or both. Which is it?"

"It... it's... complicated..."

"You write this up as suspicious or murder or whatever, but if you stick by misadventure and try to sweep this under the carpet, you'll be lying in the drawer next to him. Do you understand?"

"Yes..." Hu struggled to breathe. Most of his neck and throat was in Lomu's giant hand, like a boa constrictor gripping its prey. "I... I can't breathe..." Lomu released his grip and shoved him all the way to his desk, where he sprawled over it, scattering files and papers to the floor. "Who is paying you to write this up incorrectly?"

The door opened and Lomu looked up expecting to see a few security guards. But he hadn't counted on half a dozen police officers, some aiming Tasers through the doorway and two carrying Glock 17 pistols, with the business ends pointing directly at him.

EIGHT

They took him past oncology and he wondered just how close he was to his mother as he was pushed past the entrance. Closer than he had been for twenty years, that was for sure. He imagined her - although he could not picture her properly - sitting beside Josefa holding his hand and helping him through his chemotherapy. He had been planning to stick his head around the door when he had finished in the mortuary – he had thought a casual approach might prove easier for everybody all round - but that was academic now. Although he did wonder whether he would have made good on his intention, so perhaps it was fitting that the police hadn't given him the chance.

The cuffs were tight. On the last notch. But he did not complain and because of the width and bulk of his shoulders his arms could not be secured behind his back. One of the officers had threaded another pair of handcuffs through his belt and secured the cuffs that were around his wrists to that. The officer had smiled and confirmed in his radio that the perpetrator had been 'hog-tied'. Lomu knew that the Fijian police were not routinely armed, but they had access to modern high-tech weaponry and noted that two officers carried Glock pistols with no apparent recourse. He was loaded unceremoniously into the rear seats of a Toyota Hi-Lux pickup truck, the double cab seats offering him little in the way of headspace and legroom. He was joined by a large black Fijian in the rear, while a white man in his early thirties got behind the wheel and a woman of Indian heritage got into the front passenger seat. She was dressed in a navy trouser suit with a white blouse, and she carried a large smartphone as if it were glued to her fingers. She gave the order to drive, and that told Lomu everything he needed to know.

"Are you the detective in charge of the Hussein case?"

The woman ignored him, but not her phone. She had been swiping and typing and scrolling and she did not stop when her prisoner had spoken. She said something to the driver, but Lomu was unable to catch what she had said due to the vehicle's lumpy diesel engine and the roughness of the road surface.

"I said, are you the detective in charge of the Hussein case?" He paused. "You know, the boy who was murdered on top of Nakandua, but who everyone would rather just bumped his head by accident. But here's the news, he didn't. It was murder and you need to do your damn job."

The female detective said something else to the driver and he swung a left across the carriageway. Within a hundred metres they were travelling down a bumpy road that hadn't had a coat of tarmac in twenty years. Another left and they were on a dirt track with the city far behind them and no intention of going to the police station.

Lomu took some strain against his belt. The handcuffs held firm, and there was no way that he could break the leather, but he felt confident that he could break the buckle.

That would leave him able to defend himself, but it still didn't free both his hands. He glanced at the police officer next to him. The man had a retractable asp, or truncheon, and a cannister of CS spray on his belt. He could not see what the driver was carrying, but he knew that neither of these officers had pointed a Glock at him back at the mortuary. The detective could well be armed, but Lomu was pragmatic and had no doubt that he would show her no mercy and take her down as swiftly as the other two. He did not know whether she was armed, but even though she was slightly built, she could well present a problem if he overlooked her for the other two burly men. Although all of this was hypothetical unless he could get out of the vehicle. To break the buckle, it would require all his strength and room to move. Until then, he was about as effective as a trussed chicken.

The driver eased the pickup into a clearing fringed in palms. The ground was sandy with a myriad of short, grass patches. Lomu saw glimpses of the sea sparkling through the palms. The sun was low, only another two hours of the day remaining. The driver switched off the engine and the silence was all consuming. Lomu's heart hammered against his chest. He needed space to wrench the belt buckle hard enough to break the handcuffs free, and even then, his hands would be shackled, with another set of handcuffs hanging from them. He would need to strike first, strike hard, use his forehead and feet as well as his shackled hands, and he still did not know whether the detective was armed. She would have to go down first; there was no alternative.

The woman leaned over her seat and nodded at the officer beside Lomu, who took out a set of keys and unlocked both sets of handcuffs. Lomu frowned and rubbed his wrists. "My name is Shabnam. I'm a detective and I hold the rank of Inspector." She nodded to the man in the driver's seat. "This is Sergeant Keane, and beside you is Constable Afara." She paused. "I know you are Davinder Lomu, and you have returned to your family at Kintoto Point."

Lomu had not had anybody call him Davinder for more than half his life. When he had joined the British army, he had wanted to fit in and had said that his name was David. On account of his giant stature, he had soon been called 'Big Dave', and the name had stuck. Fiji was a melting pot of cultures and even though he was predominantly from African heritage, there was an Indian and Polynesian blood-line in the mix, too. He had been named after his maternal great grandfather, an Indian soldier in the British Army and later, a sugar plantation owner on the island. The man had lost both his standing and his assets in a series of poorly executed card games and became the black sheep of the family. Lomu's mother had revived the name in the hope of laying the past to rest, but since he had left for the United Kingdom, he had been nothing more than the black sheep, the outsider. Perhaps there was something in a name.

"What else do you know about me?"

"You served in the military. Some of your record was difficult to find, other parts were impossible." She paused, wiping her brow with a handkerchief. "It's hot in here; let's get out for a chat and then we can get you back to town."

Shabnam got out of the vehicle and tucked her blouse in where it had ridden up on the drive. Lomu could see that she was indeed armed. Beside the compact Glock 19 in a moulded plastic holster was clipped an ID wallet and a pair of handcuffs to her belt. Lomu got out and stretched, still rubbing his wrists where the handcuffs had rubbed. It had been an effort to get the hasp of the handcuffs to close on the last ratchet.

"What are we doing here?" he asked, checking that the other two men were still seated in the vehicle. "I'm either under arrest, or I'm not. And if I'm not, then fuck you and have a nice day..."

She smiled and walked a few paces away, beckoning him to join her. When he did, he could see the ocean and they both watched it as she spoke. "My boss is dirty," she said. "And his bosses, too. McGregor Enterprises own them. The two men in the pickup can be trusted. As can the vast majority of the police department, but I'm not yet sure who. McGregor has bought off enough people to get things done. The investigation quashed; the cause of death down-played." She paused, emanating a sigh. "And the search for your sister."

"You know my family?"

Shabnam smiled. "I *am* your family..." She laughed. "Well, sort of. You know what I mean. I grew up at Kintoto Point. I know your mother and Josefa, and I know Marie and Delilah. I remember your mom's banana bread," she said fondly. "My family moved to the city for work twelve years ago. I went to college and joined the police."

Lomu studied her face. He could tell a great deal by someone's eyes and expression. He trusted her, but he did not remember her, nor recognise her name. But she had to be a good eight or nine years younger than himself. Just one of the kids bursting into his house for snacks after school while he was a troubled teen mourning the loss of his father and trying to come to terms with his mother and Josefa. It was no wonder he did not remember her. "So, why are we here and not down at the police station?"

"You've come to find Monique."

"Right."

"So, find her."

"It's as easy as that…"

"And you've come to stop the development at Kintoto Point and find Mustafa's killer."

"I have?"

"That's what I've been told."

"That's more than I knew."

"So, get it done," she said curtly. "Start doing what your family got you out here to do." She paused, handing him back his mobile phone, wallet and multitool. She then took out her phone and said, "Give me your number…" He did so and she dialled. His phone rang once, and she hung up. Now you have it. Don't save it under my name. You never know who will get access to your phone." Lomu smiled. He didn't need fieldcraft tips at this level, but it showed that she was competent. "I'll help in any way I can. I have access to the police database, but I am required to sign in using my own dedicated user code, so it could be problematic, but I can use any leverage I have and be on hand to assist. Oh, and while you're at it, it would be great if you could find out who exactly McGregor has on his payroll. That would make my job a whole lot easier."

"That's it?"

"That's it."

NINE

Lomu didn't need another coroner's report to tell him that Mustafa Hussein had been murdered. What was done was done and there was a family who needed to bury a son and who struggled with the financial prospect of doing so. He found the funeral parlour on Namena Road and was told that a funeral on the island cost between $4000 and $10,000 Fijian dollars. He settled on $7000, just over £2500. He had been to enough funerals over the years to know a mid-price funeral had enough bells and whistles to feel every effort had been made to honour the deceased, but without verging on the ostentatious. He also knew this was still half the price his former comrades' families had paid in the UK. It was sad, he thought, that so many people he had known had survived military conflict but had died soon after in civilian life through poor life choices or suicide. He used his own debit card, reflecting that if he was going to step up and make such a gesture, then he would give MI5 a break and dip into his own funds. He did not have much in the way of savings, and now he had a lot less.

Once he had made the payment and instructed the

funeral director to contact the mortuary and Mustafa's family to make the necessary arrangements and made the funeral director promise not to disclose who had paid, Lomu headed back to Kintoto Point on the coast road. He was tired and jet lagged and hungry. Known as 'Big Dave' not only for his size and stature, but for his voracious appetite, he normally ate five meals a day. Marie's battered fish pieces, tasty as they were, had only teased his appetite, and he pulled over at a shack selling beach toys, ice cream and fruit. He ambled over and perused the table, settling on a half shell of fresh king coconut filled with various fruits and topped with coconut cream. It came with a single-use wooden spoon, and he perched back on the warm bonnet of the Jeep and ate while he watched the ocean below. The coconut had been loosened from the shell and the rich coconut cream – blended coconut flesh and coconut milk – made the entire experience one of decadence, yet thoroughly healthy and wholesome. It was the best fruit and coconut he had eaten in twenty-years. He tucked in hungrily. His usual diet was generally fried and consisted of fifty percent meat. The other fifty percent was made up from bread and potatoes. He had always countered the nutrition argument with his workouts and runs, but he knew it couldn't last forever. The credit and debit system he had used thus far with his health had worked, but he knew that it wasn't going to work forever, and he needed to embrace healthier food as he crashed headlong into middle age. He looked out over the ocean and the setting sun, spooning in another mouthful of this ambrosia nectar and started to feel at home for the first time in two decades. Food like this tasted better in a place like this. Britain, with its damp and drizzle, its cold winds and torrential rain called for warming pies, steaming piles of fish and chips, cakes and an inexhaustible supply of biscuits to take with tea or coffee.

The pickup pulled in recklessly, throwing dust and chippings in the air. Lomu covered his coconut bowl with his giant paw, but it was too late. The pure white creamed coconut was covered with a layer of dust and dirt and debris as thoroughly as a chef would sprinkle tiramisu with cocoa powder. Lomu stared at it, then looked up to see two men striding towards him, one carrying a baseball bat and the other carrying a crowbar. Lomu didn't move as he studied both men. Regular guys, regular build. But they were coming in hot. Lomu waited for them to get to within eight feet, and he pitched the coconut shell at the man with the baseball bat, as he took two strides forwards, caught hold of the crowbar and headbutted the other man on the bridge of his nose. He went down hard, releasing his grip on the crowbar as he fell. The other man had stopped in his tracks. He now held the baseball bat in one hand as he picked the fruit from his face. It all looked so comical, but the coconut shell had sliced into his face with terrific force, and he was bleeding from the bridge of his nose and was tentatively feeling his eyes where some of the coconut shell had ended up. Lomu wasted no time driving the crowbar into the man's balls, then swiped it across his left shin for good measure. The man howled and fell onto his side. He clutched his shin in one hand and cupped his balls in the other, his face a mess of blood and coconut cream and tropical fruits. He panted for breath and sucked in air through gritted teeth.

"That's gotta hurt," said Lomu pointedly.

"Fuck you..." the man managed.

"Who sent you?"

"Fuck you..."

Lomu nodded. "That pickup belong to you or McGregor?"

"What's it to do with you?"

"I'm figuring McGregor is a wealthy man and won't miss a truck when I roll it off the cliff." He paused. "But if it's yours, then I'm also figuring that you're not going to want me to do that." The man stared up at him, miraculously the pain ebbing as he took on this new development. "But then again, perhaps McGregor will hold you responsible and you'll end up owing him for the truck. I'm guessing Mitsubishi trucks aren't cheap."

Lomu stepped past the man and headed for the truck. On his way, he nudged his right foot underneath the unconscious man and rolled him onto his side. He could see that he was breathing, but in the words of his old unarmed combat instructor, had gone 'night-night'. Rolling him onto his side would stop the man from choking on his own tongue, as well as any blood and mucus that would be clotting in the man's nose and nasal passages. The bed of the truck was loaded with lobster and crab pots, rope, nets, flags and buoys. He looked back at the men on the ground. The man with the face full of coconut was now sitting on his backside and wiping the shell from his eyes. These men were fishermen, or at least earned some extra dollars dropping lobster pots, which they no doubt sold to the hotels and restaurants in the area. They may well have worked for McGregor, but he doubted the developer would allow one of his trucks to be used for personal endeavours such as fishing. Lomu tossed the crowbar over the edge of the cliff and opened the door of the pickup. He slipped the gearbox into neutral and took off the handbrake. The truck remained where it was. He looked at the man who was now getting to his feet. The man stared back, then when he realised what

Lomu was about to do, he limped towards him, waving his hands to stop him.

"No! Don't do it!" the man begged. "It's my livelihood, man!" Lomu put his back into it, eighteen stone making short work of getting the truck moving on the flat surface. The truck eased forwards two feet, steadily gaining in speed. "No!"

Lomu pulled the handbrake and the wheels locked, skidding on the gravel. "Who sent you?"

"I can't man..." the man paused. "I'll end up cemented into the foundations..."

Lomu released the brake and the truck started moving again, this time he had to walk quickly to keep up.

"No!"

Lomu pulled the handbrake. "Then tell me who sent you!"

The man shrugged. "Carter..."

Lomu stared at the man, but without seeing him. He was picturing the Australian both at the development, and again, standing on the embankment with a gun in his hand while three of his stooges did his dirty work for him. And now two more. He looked at the cliff and the drop to the rocks below. The man was hovering, watching Lomu and watching the fate of his vehicle. Lomu knew that if he did not send the truck off the edge of the cliff, then it could be construed as weakness. However, these men were hard workers and needed the extra money that fishing brought them. Were they really a further threat to him? He wondered what the other members of his team would have done in his place. There was no doubt that King would have already pulled the handbrake – most probably dragged the two men back into the truck to give them a one-way ride onto the rocks below. Caroline would have been more objective, most likely erred on the side of caution and shown the same clemency as he was tempted to display. Although, there was no telling what headspace she would be in after recent events. Rashid? A closed book as far as he was concerned, impossible to read. But all Lomu knew was that he was his own man, and right now, it felt the right thing to do. He stepped away and walked back to the Jeep.

"Thank you," the man said quietly, taking a few steps backwards to remain distanced from Lomu.

"If you come after me again, then I'll kill you," he replied.

"We won't, man."

"See that you don't."

TEN

With the setting sun suspended just above the horizon, the ocean glistening with the last embers of sunlight, and the stars already on display in the sky far to the east, Lomu pulled into the Kintoto Point community and parked near Marie's bure. There were dozens of children, some playing, others seemingly running chores. Many carried bowls and dishes and were heading towards the beach. Lomu switched off the engine and watched Marie step out onto the veranda, wiping her hands on a cloth, an apron wrapped around her and tied at her trim waist.

"About time," she said. "Mom's home. Are you ready?"

"For what?" he replied, closing the door of the Jeep and walking towards her.

"You haven't seen her in twenty years, and the last time you were here you were acting like an idiot." She paused. "It's kind of a big deal for everyone that you're home. Stop resisting, swallow your damn pride and be on your best behaviour."

Lomu shrugged. "No pressure then..." He turned his

eyes to the stream of children ferrying bowls and plates, then looked back at his sister. "What's going on?"

Marie smiled. "Dinner."

"It looks a bit more than dinner."

She shrugged. "Well, OK, it started out that way, but kind of turned into a feast. We started off with steamed fish in banana leaves, coconut rice and taro, then before we knew it, Peter killed a pig and..."

"Poor pig," Lomu commented.

"Oh, so I suppose you've been in the Western world long enough to forget where your food comes from," she teased. "Anyway, it was just a small pig." Lomu nodded, although he couldn't see any logic in the justification. So now they were eating a baby pig... He looked towards the beach where bamboo torches tied with oil-soaked wadding had been speared into the sand and lit as was tradition with feasts, the flames flickering in the warm breeze. He felt anxious, nervous. As strange as it seemed, he was as nervous as he'd ever been going into battle. The thought of seeing his own mother after all this time, let alone Josefa, suddenly seemed real and unavoidable. Bar turning around and driving to the airport, this was going to happen. Seeing his hesitation, Marie caught hold of his hand and led him towards the beach. "Come on, Davy. She's missed you. Everybody has..."

Lomu nodded. So now it was time. Stubbornness had kept him away for so long, his pride increasing the gulf between them perceptively more than the ten-thousand miles of ocean and land. He followed Marie through the settlement and onto the sand. The table had been constructed as it always had for special occasions – several similar tables put end to end, and the legs tied together with twine to stop the individual tables shifting. Sheets adorned the tables and salads, fruit, rice, taro and sweet potato dishes held the sheets in place in the evening breeze. Several men manned the grill, the coals glowing brightly in the darkness, great slabs of fish marinated in coriander, coconut and limes broiled on the grill and skewers of prawns still in their shells licked by the flames sizzled and changed from translucent grey and blue to candy red. Another group of men were unwrapping a suckling pig (killed by Peter – but just a small one) that had been seasoned with salt and pepper and chopped fresh mint, stuffed with jackfruit and wrapped tightly in banana leaves before being placed on glowing embers and hot rocks and buried in the sand. The real skill was in getting the banana leaves off without sand getting onto the meat. It took three men and a great deal of opinion from many onlookers to get the job done. Lomu was taken back to his childhood as he surveyed the scene. This was how his extended family celebrated weddings and birthdays and Christmas, and a dozen holidays in between.

"Bula!" a man said, pounding up to Lomu greeting him enthusiastically with a half shell of coconut. "Kava!" He thrust the local brew, a truly acquired taste, into Lomu's hand and watched expectantly as Lomu drank the liquid down in one go, as was expected of him.

"Bula!" Lomu replied, as was tradition to say 'hello' in Fijian. He was no fan of kava – the drink made from the dried yaqona root. The fact that 'kava' meant bitter in neighbouring Tonga would tell one all there is to know about the traditional Fijian drink that made its way into every Fijian celebration.

The man smiled and thrust a bottle of Fosters into Lomu's hand and grinned as he appreciatively drained half the beer, although his mouth was starting to go numb, and he felt as if he'd had several beers already, such was the strength of the kava. The man returned to the grill in time to turn the prawns, laughing with a teenaged boy who was learning the art of grilling.

Lomu walked onwards, following Marie, his feet leaden and his pace slowing as he grew ever closer to the inevitable. Marie turned and beckoned him forwards, annoyed that he was lagging behind. As he approached the table, all eyes turned on him. He always tended to draw looks with his stature and presence when he entered a room, and as he approached the table, it was no different here. Not, he reflected, the most subtle of people for undercover work with Britain's leading anti-terrorism and counter espionage unit, but he always got the job done.

Marie saw their mother seated with her back to them and hurried over. Feeling Lomu lagging hesitantly behind, she caught hold of his hand and pulled him as best she could. The old woman looked round and Lomu's heart sank. He had left it too long. Too many years had passed aimlessly, and for what? Pride? Stubbornness? He realised he had lost the woman he had known as his mother and instead, an old woman sat before him, sadness worn into her face. And yet. A glimmer of recognition, of happiness sparkled in her eyes. She struggled to get up, overcome with emotion, but Marie helped her to her feet, and she hugged her boy for the first time in over twenty years. Lomu said nothing. He just felt the warmth and familiarity wash over him. He found himself closing his eyes and soaking it up. When he opened them again, Josefa, who was seated opposite, had got to his feet and smiled warmly at him. Lomu remembered the man being taller, but then he realised it was because he had still had two years growing to do after he had left for Britain. He looked the man in the eyes, which he rarely did to another man. Six-feet-four was tall

all around the world, and although he occasionally met a man who was taller, he generally looked down on everybody he met. Lomu's mother pulled him back down, hugging him closely.

"Let the boy breathe, Mindy..." Josefa chided her. He beckoned Lomu to sit down beside his mother, then looked each way down the table and banged his fist loudly on the tabletop several times, causing everyone nearby to stop talking and stare over. "Our guest is here!" he announced. Lomu would swear the man seemed proud somehow. "Now we can all eat!"

Excited children found chairs while the adults made space for the food and sat down to help themselves to the salads, fruits and vegetables while several men walked their platters over and placed them in front of expectant eyes. The feast was in full flow within a minute and Marie sat down with her children and everyone bunched up for new arrivals. Lomu looked up and saw Delilah with a young white man in his late twenties. They looked very much in love, with that hesitant resistance to break being a couple and mingle with a group, that relationships in their infancy often had.

"Don't leave it so long next time, boy," Mindy said sharply.

Lomu shrugged. "I was hurt. I needed time to heal."

"Are you done?" He shrugged again but couldn't think what else to say. "You have a sister you've never met..." She trailed off, then said, "Oh my, this feels so wrong, celebrating with Monique still missing and all..."

Josefa walked around the table and she went to him, hugging him closely as she sobbed. Lomu felt redundant and sipped from his bottle of beer. He could not comfort her. Who was he to do that? Josefa had been here all these years, her constant companion. He sat down and helped himself from a plate of shredded pork. Marie heaped on mashed sweet potato boiled in coconut milk, and Delilah passed him some taro. He hadn't eaten food like this in twenty years and he was salivating. Within a few mouthfuls, he was bitterly disappointed. His tastes had changed. Thai seemed far more fragrant, while Indian cuisine elevated everything with its heavy use of butter and spices. The pork was good, though. He shovelled in mouthfuls as his mother took her seat once more and Josefa made his way – somewhat unsteadily – back around the table.

"I loved your father dearly..." his mother started, but Josefa cut her off.

"You don't need to justify yourself, my dear. Davinder is a grown man. He can either accept what we have had over the years, or he can leave us be..." He looked at Lomu and said, "I am pleased that you are here, but we don't apologise for anything, because we did nothing wrong. We love each other, and we both loved your..." He paused, swallowing painfully. Lomu reflected that the man did not look well, and that he had only had chemotherapy treatment this afternoon. "... father and both mourned his passing."

Lomu nodded. He didn't see it like that, even after all these years, but he wasn't going to make a scene. He turned to his mother and clasped her hand in his own. "I understand," he said softly. "I'm just glad that I am here and I'm happy to help."

"Seems you've started helping already," said Delilah. "Mustafa Hussein's funeral was paid for anonymously. Seems the man who paid fitted your description and spoke in a *London* accent. The boy may have forgotten his roots, but he still has style..."

"Really Davinder?" Mindy asked her son. "Is this true?"

"Must be somebody else," he replied gruffly as he loaded more pork onto his plate.

"He was a good boy," Josefa commented flatly. He raised his glass. Lomu thought it must have been water. The dim light and flickering flames of the torches made it difficult to see. Josefa toasted loudly, "To Mustafa!" Most people in the vicinity reciprocated his toast and drank to it with everything from beer to kava to wine. When he had finished his drink, Josefa smiled at Mindy and said, "Monique will be fine, my dear. She has her mother's spirit. She will endure."

"You're convinced that she's still alive?" Lomu asked, although he realised his tone hadn't been at all sympathetic.

"Of course!" his mother snapped.

Lomu nodded. Of course, she would.

"We've only put all this on for you, Davy," Marie explained. "We'd all be in our bures moping around, like we have since she disappeared, if you weren't here, and if mom hadn't insisted..."

He shrugged. "So, what have you done to find her?" he asked.

"We have searched the area where Mustafa's body was found." Delilah paused, glancing at Mindy and Josefa. She could see the hurt in their eyes, the suspension of belief and the clinging of hope. "And we went out to Uluwala, the island where Mustafa and Monique went out to in their search to prove that Kintoto Point is sacred ground and halt the development. They were adamant that if they found the talisman, then they would find the answer to our problem. The church on Uluwala has many Fijian artifacts in a small museum, and Mustafa heard about a piece of jewellery that was found recently and carbon dated. It's old. Like BC. Anyway, as you may remember, it was one of the seven islands where Degei is said to be lying, awaiting the time of resurrection. Degei the serpent god, and the supreme god, judges the newly dead souls to pass through two caves for the afterlife. These caves are Cibaciba or Drakula. Some souls are sent to paradise, called Burotu. Most are thrown into a lake and sink to the bottom, called Murimuria where they will be appropriately rewarded, or punished."

Lomu nodded. "I remember the teachings. I left Fiji, but I didn't forget my past." He paused. "And the talisman is a myth. We're not going to find it."

"Why not?" Josefa asked indignantly.

"Because it's like finding The Arc of the Covenant."

"No. It's like finding the talisman of Degei. I don't believe in the god of the Bible, or the Quran. I believe in Fiji's traditions and culture." Josefa paused. "It's called faith, because to believe in a god is a choice, and the ultimate test of faith."

"From a man called Josefa..."

"My parents were Muslim, and they named me as such. But I chose my beliefs. Besides, it's only a name. I hear that nobody knows you as Davinder in Britain. You have your reasons for that, I am sure."

Lomu glanced at Delilah, who looked away. She had obviously told them about the journey from the airport. He shrugged at Josefa. "I suppose," he replied.

"Marie has told me that you have come here to help," Josefa said. "For that, I thank you. Tell me, what can you do that we cannot, and what will you do first?"

Lomu finished his beer and placed the bottle on the table. Delilah handed him another and he placed it beside the empty bottle. "I have some experience finding people," he replied. He did not think that it was necessary to tell them about the Al Qaeda and ISIS terrorists he had found and tracked and eliminated while he was with the SAS. He had been given an unprecedented loose rein on that operation. His later work with MI5 often required him to fit a detective role. "I'm here to help, and I won't leave until we have answers."

Marie left the table saying she would fetch some more vegetable dishes and Delilah got up to help her.

Mindy squeezed her son's hand. "They have been wonderful, but it is taking its toll not knowing what has become of Monique." She paused. "Your own half-sister, a young woman now, and you have not yet met her..." She trailed off, wondering if he ever would.

Lomu looked away. He could not explain the emotion he was feeling for a young girl whom he had never met, had not known her existence until just a week ago. He had tried to downplay it with both Marie and Delilah, but it was simply there. The family bond. The feeling that you would risk everything to help and be damned with the consequences. As a distraction, and not drawing attention to his mother who was drying her eyes with a tissue, he helped himself to yet more pork. The meat was succulent and melted in the mouth. He spooned on more sweet potato and suddenly got the cuisine in that instant. It may have lacked the sophistication of Thai or the depth of flavour of Indian cuisine, but it was homely, comforting. It made the best of what was to hand, and consisted of dishes that filled a family's stomach, cost little and enabled people to get through a day's toil. He realised that he had missed it, but perhaps that also had something to do with being 'home'. He looked around him. Family, extended family and friends. All celebrating his return, even though one of their own was missing, and the development threatened their very existence. If the development at Kintoto Point went ahead, then these families would disperse and likely be forced into the towns and city and a way of life would be lost forever, consigned to Fiji's history.

Lomu looked back at his mother. He could see her features more clearly and he noticed how old she seemed compared to his memories of her. He turned to Josefa, the man's features becoming clearer in the light. The light brightening every second, until Lomu realised that he was in fact in the centre of a beam of light. He glanced to his right, just as the vehicle caught the side of one of the huts and smashed its way through, the headlights now shining directly on Josefa and turning night into day. Lomu swept up his mother in his hands, the vehicle looming down on them, he kicked the table as hard as he could and Josefa was barrelled over, still in his chair and he rolled backwards onto the sand, just as the pickup truck smashed into the table end on and ploughed through the entire family gathering scattering chairs and splintering the three tethered tables. Food, crockery and cutlery went everywhere, and inevitably, some people were broadsided by the careening vehicle. Lomu looked at Josefa. The man was getting to his feet, shaken, bruised, but the truck had thankfully missed him.

Lomu ran his mother to Marie's house. It was a sturdier construction to the nearer bures, and he sprinted with her in his arms, aware that the pickup truck was turning around on the beach, giant rooster tails of sand being thrown up behind it. There were more trucks coming, and gunshots rang-out from somewhere inside the camp. Lomu darted inside, dropped his mother onto a worn cloth sofa and saw Marie on her mobile phone.

"I'm calling the police!" she screamed, then tutted as she ended the call and dialled again. "Damn it!" This time, she got straight through and started to explain to the operator what had happened.

Lomu's eyes rested on the shotgun above the mantel. He strode over, snatched it down and turned to Marie. "Do you have shells for this?"

Marie pointed at the dresser. "Top drawer!" she shouted.

The shotgun was a single barrel, single shot affair with a hammer to cock the weapon and a thumb latch to break open the action. He pulled out the drawer and snatched a handful of 12-bore cartridges. He had the weapon loaded and made ready before he got to the door, and he shot out the windscreen of an approaching pickup as he stepped out onto the veranda. He reloaded and watched the truck veer away and onto the beach. The gunshots he had heard were that of a medium calibre pistol and he could see the muzzle flashes as bright as day with every report. He aimed the shotgun at the muzzle flash and fired. There was a terrific scream and the pickup lurched sideways and tore through a bure and left nothing but matchwood and straw in its wake. He reloaded, ran down onto the beach and caught hold of Josefa, who was looking dazed and confused, having just dodged another pickup truck. It wasn't the evening the doctors thought he would have after an afternoon of chemotherapy. Lomu raced back to Marie's bure, pulling the man behind him. Lomu noted that for his tall stature, the man was surprisingly light and rangy. Emaciated, even. No doubt eaten away by the cancer he was being treated for. Mindy leapt up and hugged Josefa close, exclaiming how happy she was that he was alright. But others were not, and Lomu left them in the bure and headed for the screaming coming from the beach. He kept the weapon ready, but the distant taillights told him that the trucks were no longer a threat, and he de-cocked the shotgun then broke open the breach, pocketing the shell.

Several men crowded round a woman who was scream-ing, but Lomu knew enough about battlefield triage to know that a woman screaming at the top of her lungs wasn't necessarily a priority. He scoured the beach, discounting the clearly dead from the quiet. He checked the pulse of a young man lying on his back, but he had gone. He hesitated, conflicted as to whether he should try CPR, but there was something about the eerie stillness that told him to pass. Next to him an older woman lay twisted and broken, her head resting at an impossible angle. Lomu continued. When he found the woman, he knew he had to act quickly. He hollered for assistance, taking off his belt and looping it before running it up the woman's leg just above the knee. Judging from the amount of blood on the sand, she had lost a great deal of blood from the compound fracture just below her knee. He remembered the medical courses he had been on, and the indicator of blood on various surfaces. A wooden laminate floor, for instance, with no gaps to absorb the blood, could look horrific even if it was just half a pint. A thick carpet may make the blood loss look less dramatic, but in truth there could be half the casualty's blood soaked into the underlay. Naturally, given the theatre of British military operation over two decades, sand was the surface they had concentrated upon, and Lomu knew that the woman was in trouble. He cinched the belt with the buckle and tucked the excess so that the tourniquet held firm, before moving the woman onto her side. A man appeared beside them and Lomu asked if an ambulance had been called.

"Yeah, Davinder, man. And 'tho police, too..." he

replied, his accent somewhere between Jamaica and Mumbai.

"Take off your shirt," Lomu instructed him, and when the man obliged, he rolled it up and tucked it under the woman's head. Lomu looked back at the man, realising he was his uncle. His mother's brother. It was becoming surreal.

The flashing blue, white and red lights penetrated the night and reflected off the calm, glassy ocean. Lomu told his uncle to get an ambulance over to them, and the old man got up and trudged across the sand waving his hands at the approaching lights. Lomu felt the woman's pulse. It was weak. She had lost a lot of blood. Delilah rushed over and as the two paramedics rushed across the sand, she started to fill them in with the casualty's name and medical history. Lomu stood back and surveyed the scene, reminded of battles he had been caught in. The carnage, the eerie quietness that ensued. The police were here now, and people were gathering around uniformed officers, who were caught between taking statements and looking for a senior officer to make some sense of what was going on. And then Lomu saw her. Shabnam closed the door to a white Toyota Corolla and took out her detective credentials and hung them around her neck on a lanyard. She held a notepad and pen and Lomu could see through the strobing lights and hastily erected lighting – which looked like the light bulbs mechanics often clipped under the bonnet of a vehicle that they were working on – which had been clamped to some of the smaller palm trees between the bures.

Marie and Delilah appeared at his shoulder. "Momma and Paps are okay, Kalara is sitting with them," Marie assured him. "I've made them all coffee..."

"Paps?"

She shrugged. "He's been good to me," she said. "Hey, I'm four years younger than you; he was there when I needed him, has been ever since."

Lomu nodded. He knew that he shouldn't have commented; he hadn't been here for her, and he knew he should have been grateful that his sister had support when she needed it. No matter his reasons at the time for leaving, he realised that he was the one who had turned his back on his family, and he supposed he should be thankful that they made such an effort for his return, even if it was at the behest of his sister. He caught Shabnam's eye, and she walked over. Both Delilah and Marie greeted her, although Lomu thought a little stiffly, and gave a potted account of what had happened and that they all knew who was responsible. Shabnam warned them that without proof, they could wind up in trouble making unsubstantiated accusations. Marie told her that she had to check on her family and left for her bure. Delilah made her excuses and left, leaving just Lomu and the detective standing and observing the last of the ambulances leaving, with blues and twos penetrating both the darkness and silence of the night.

"Can't go accusing people without proof," she said.

"No?"

"No."

"I shot one of them," he said. "Shotgun. Looked like birdshot."

"You shot one of them?" she glared.

"Someone offed some rounds. Nine-millimetre, I'd bet. There's a pretty good chance you'll find some ejected cases with a metal detector. That is, if they didn't eject into the vehicle. Either way, there'll be powder residue in the vehicle."

"You're assuming we have a CSI unit to match the FBI..."

"You're a detective, so go and detect!"

"I know my job!" she snapped.

"Then go do it!" Lomu shook his head. "There are at least two pickup trucks out there with damage to them, blood traces and one of them will at least have powder residue, shotgun shot rattling about inside and the guy's blood splattered on the dash. If you don't get lucky, then run the number of registered pickups. If someone has ditched theirs, then that's a red flag right there. They will have some awkward questions to answer." He paused, watching the uniformed police officers fencing off much of the area with police tape. "I reckon McGregor Enterprises will have two missing pickups," he ventured.

"McGregor brought a great deal of equipment over from his headquarters in Australia. Much of the plant equipment and many of the vehicles aren't even registered for the road. So, they don't need tax, individual insurance or safety inspections. If it was two of these vehicles, then we would never know."

"So, if two unregistered vehicles turn up ditched some-where, then you'll know who they likely belonged to," he replied. "But I suppose McGregor has probably had them buried already. Think about it. Dig a hole, run them through the village like a stampede in the Old West, then ditch them in the hole and have an excavator fill them in."

Shabnam nodded. "I'll get a team into the development at first light," she said decisively as she watched Marie leaving with a plate of food covered with foil, Delilah seeming to console her as she headed for her tiny SUV.

"When did it last rain here?"

She shrugged. "Three days ago, maybe four. Why?"

"They are still on a shutdown order, so no digging will have been going on. Filling in a hole will leave darker, moister soil on top. Don't leave it too late before you pay a visit, or the soil will have dried in the sun. you want a team in there just before dawn."

She shook her head. "Not enough time. I'll need a judge's order."

"So, get one."

"You've clearly never woken a judge up before daylight..." She looked at him and grinned. "I don't suppose you'll be taking a walk tomorrow morning, will you? Say, just before daylight?"

Lomu smiled. "Do you know, I seem to remember thinking I'd do exactly that."

ELEVEN

In March the sun rose in Fiji at 06:10. A little earlier on the island of Taveuni, one of the few places on Earth where one could straddle the International Date Line and step backwards and forwards in time by an entire day. Lomu had often reflected that he had chosen to live in the United Kingdom – not that he had spent much time there during the years he had served in the British Army – and that only New Zealand was further away from his adopted home. A quick look at the weather app on his iPhone told him that it would be a dry day, with a high of 33°c. That would dry out freshly dug earth in a matter of an hour or so once the sun was up. But he had plenty of time as it was not yet 05:30 and he had scoured the ground in the development for the past hour using the beam of a dull torch. Enough light to see by, but not enough to attract attention. That was the plan, at least.

Lomu had searched an area of around five acres, but he could not see any sign of disturbed earth. By the time the sun had come up he had searched over half the development site. He looked back at the sea, the rising sun nestled between two peaks and casting its light directly upon Kintoto Point. He had always marvelled at the sight and remembered his father telling him, *"This place is blessed because the first light of day is trapped by the mountains, but when the sun breaks free, it shines on Kintoto first, and for the longest..."* Lomu had later heard that the great British industrial and civil engineer, Isambard Kingdom Brunel had designed a railway tunnel so exactly, that the sun shone through on his birthday, at the exact time he was born. That seemed like quite a feat, but Mother Nature had seen fit to see that Kintoto Point caught the morning sunlight every single day. He looked back to the mountains, and particularly Nakandua, the sacred mountain. What had Mustafa and Monique discovered there? What had they stumbled upon, that would see one of them killed and the other disappeared, possibly dead? He had never met the girl, but the thought that something had happened to his own flesh and blood made him emotional – somewhere between rage and grief and frustration. He turned his eyes back to the ground and continued in his search. After an hour, he knew it was a bust. The best possible locations to bury a couple of pickup trucks were in the centre of the site. Any further into the mountainside and digging would be difficult. Any nearer the perimeter would have proved too risky. By eight AM, the ground was baked dry and Lomu knew he would prove nothing by hanging around. He returned to the beach, stripped off his open shirt and shorts and waded into the ocean wearing just a pair of briefs. The water was cool and refreshing, the air temperature already in the high twenties. He waded out to his waist, then dived under and swam out a hundred metres in a steady crawl. When he was in the channel, he took a breath and dived down, periodically holding his nose and blowing to equalise the pressure mounting in his ears. With every few feet he descended; the water cooled further. At twenty-five to thirty feet, he started to run out of air, and he turned in a gentle somersault and kicked for the surface. When he breached, he gasped for air and bobbed on the surface while he got his breath back. He glanced at his watch – a heavy-duty G-Shock that had seen him through years of military service in the most inhospitable places on earth. He had often thought it time to buy a premium brand like an Omega, a Breitling or a Tag Heuer, and often wiled away the waiting time in airport duty free lounges looking at the array of shiny and expensive timepieces, but his mantra had always been 'if it ain't broke, don't fix it' and the scratched and beaten G-Shock had seen him through some tough times without letting him down. Lomu figured he could get some breakfast and head into the capital, where he wanted to get some background information on Fijian heritage and history and see if he could work out what both Mustafa and Monique had discovered. He was doubtful of the worthiness of his plan, but it was start.

Lomu swam along the edge of the channel, a favourite place of his to swim all those years ago. And for good reason. He took a deep breath and dived down again, this time his ears needing less equalising as he swam down into the depths. The sandy bottom gave way to rock on the edge of the channel, and he saw a flicker of movement and swam harder. Although his eyes were blurred from the saltwater, he could see the black and red and blue of the spiny lobster heading for the rocks. He swam hard, snatched out his right hand and caught hold of the lobster by its carapace. The crustacea protested by whipping its antenna and working its legs, curling its tail in the manner females did to protect their roe. It was a sizeable catch, at least two kilos in weight, and almost as thick around as his forearm. One of the things Lomu liked most about this species of lobster was its lack of claws. He could cope with being whipped by its antenna as he swam to the surface and headed back to shore swimming sidestroke, just as he had as a youth foraging the lagoon for dinner. He was pleased that he still had the skills he had honed so many years ago, but even more pleased that he would be having a simple, yet hearty breakfast of grilled lobster and butter. As he stroked somewhat awkwardly to shore, he remembered how his father and Josefa had taught him and the other boys to catch lobster. Always an hour after dawn, when the sharks had eaten their fill from their night-time feeding activity and the lobsters came out from the ledges and crevices to feed, and always with the sun on your back to hide within the creature's light-sensitive vision. Like a kamikaze pilot divebombing a vessel while the sailors on board squint helplessly into the sun.

When he felt the sand on his toes, his screw kick from his sidestroke touching down a little deeper than he would normally have, he got to his feet and waded through the gentle surf, the waves no larger than the wake a small craft would create on a lake. Rapid and constant, which told Lomu that the surf on the outer reefs would be huge today. When he looked back at the beach, Carter stood dominantly on the sand, his hands on hips. He was flanked by a Fijian on either side. He had brought the big guns with him today. The back row of a rugby team, both men the size of Lomu, and he noted as he walked towards them without pausing a beat, possibly even larger.

"Mister McGregor would like you to join him for breakfast," Carter told him, his Australian accent twangy and distinct in the early morning silence. Lomu thought he sounded like a strangled cat.

Lomu held up the lobster and shrugged. "I've got breakfast plans," he replied. He subconsciously rubbed the bullet wound to his shoulder, which had started to ache from the swim. He noticed Carter smile and he could have cursed himself for his own stupidity. You never showed weakness to the enemy.

"I'd advise you to come with us."

Lomu shrugged. "Or what?"

"Don't make this more difficult than it has to be," Carter replied. "Mister McGregor has recognised that you're a bloke not to be pushed, so he would like to meet you, have some coffee and eggs and talk about the development starting up smoothly, and how to move forward with no further delays." He held up his hands. "No guns, no violence."

Lomu noted that he still wore the Bowie knife on his belt, and the fact that the two men weren't there merely for decoration. He weighed up his options. To refuse would likely end in a fight, and even though he could handle himself, they had more than double the muscle, pound for pound. He had taught unarmed combat in the SAS, and from that experience he knew that nothing was for certain in a fight. But he also knew that he would be going around in circles if he simply walked away, whether he beat the other men or not. The way he saw it, McGregor was behind the development, and whatever Mustafa and Monique had discovered had led to one of them being killed and the other going missing.

Lomu looked at the lobster in his hand, the two-foot-long pair of antennae still whipping back and forth catching his leg. He tossed the creature back into the ocean and watched as it took off backwards like a torpedo. "It's your lucky day, fella," he said quietly, before picking up his shirt and shaking off the sand as he stepped into his new pair of flip-flops. "Go on, then..." He paused. "Lead the way..."

Carter nodded, but Lomu sensed he was doing his best to suppress a grin. The man certainly looked like the cat who'd got the cream. Neither of the hulking giants beside him batted an eye. It was just business for them; they hadn't been needed, but they would get paid anyway. Lomu gave the men a wide berth as he followed Carter to the black Range Rover Vogue with impossibly dark tinted windows. He took a rear seat. Carter sat beside him, and the muscle rode up front. Lomu could not tell the two men apart, but one of them drove and the other didn't. Lomu glanced at Carter's knife, sheathed and hanging from his belt. It was a large Bowie, and he estimated the blade to be north of ten inches. The handle was made from antler with a brass cross-guard and pommel. It must have weighed six or seven pounds, and he noted that a series of notches had been nicked out of one side of the leather sheath.

Interesting.

"What have you done with the girl?" Lomu asked, watching Carter closely for a response.

"Nothing."

"Do you *know* what has happened to her?"

"No."

Strangely, Lomu believed him. "And the boy?" he ventured.

Carter stared at him. "Just what are you doing here?"

Evasive.

"I'm seeing my family."

"You left a long time ago, Lomu."

"You seem to know a lot about me."

"Forewarned is forearmed."

"Well, there's always the unexpected."

"You don't know what you're getting into," Carter replied flippantly. "I've seen how this pans out for people like you." He paused, a smirk cracking his cruel-looking lips. "You're a tall man, Lomu. But you're out of your depth."

"I'll take my chances."

Carter scoffed indignantly. "You don't really care about those peasants back there. You're here because of some misguided sense of duty that nags at you because you left and lived your life how you wanted to. No, you don't *really* care." Carter paused, the vehicle leaving the rough surface for a smooth service road of compressed hardcore and gravel. "If you did, then you would have known that you had a half-sister, let alone another half a dozen extra cousins. Jesus, they're just a bunch of gypsies. You got out. I commend that. You're better than them."

"You seem to know a lot about my family. Or think you do," Lomu replied tersely. "And for the record; gypsies are travelling people. My family have done everything they can to stay at the point for hundreds of years. It's my family's heritage. You really are as stupid as you look..."

Carter stared at him. "Careful, mate. You don't want to get on the wrong side of me..."

"Like Mustafa and Monique?" Lomu countered.

"You don't know what the fuck you're talking about."

"Listen, Crocodile Dundee, if there's a bad mother fucker on this island who doesn't need getting on the wrong side of, then it's me..." He watched in silence as the service road gave way to tarmac and the Range Rover made swift progress along the coast road but soon taking a steep slipway that took them high above the coast and into the mountains. Thankfully Carter hadn't batted back a repost, Lomu felt he would have simply pulled out the man's throat rather than continue with a verbal back and forward. He glanced at the knife, noticing that the leather clip securing the handle had been unfastened. He'd missed that and realised that the notches on the sheath were there for a reason. He wouldn't miss a detail like that again. And if each notch really did stand for a life, then he would bet anything that Carter hadn't faced many of his opponents eye to eye, not at the end at least.

The pickup slowed and they took a right off the road and onto a track. Like the service road, the track was well compressed and smooth. Palms lined the verges and neatly manicured lawns with stripes mown so perfectly that the gardener could have secured a groundsman post at Lords. After a hundred metres they rounded a righthand bend and a colonial style house loomed in the distance. Painted white and with typical colonial covered balustrades on all sides, the only splash of colour came from the terracotta tiled roof. A single figure stood in the centre of the third-floor balustrade dressed in white and wearing a Panama hat. Lomu watched the man watching him. The man exuded authority and confidence, then as the Range Rover pulled to a halt, Lomu looked at the sneer upon the man's face. Disdain. Arrogance. Indifference. Lomu couldn't decide which, then settled on all three.

"Out," Carter ordered.

Lomu kept a wary eye on the knife as he opened the door and stepped out onto a paved driveway that must have consisted of three-thousand or more paver bricks. Red like the terracotta roof tiles. When he looked back up at the top balcony the man had disappeared.

Sinister.

"This way..." Carter snapped and led the way across the driveway and up eight marble steps, where the enormous oak door was already open. The two giants held back, hovering at the threshold like the floor was lava. Carter shot them a look and they remained either side of the door like fortress guards.

Inside, the house was airy and lace curtains moved lazily in the through-breeze. The furnishings were largely colonial, with heavy, dark wooden cabinets, tables and book-shelves, yet with modern bamboo furniture fitted with floral cushions. There were animal head trophies on the walls and Lomu was drawn to that of a lion's head, replete with mane.

"The boss shot that big bastard," said Carter.

"Brave man," Lomu commented sarcastically.

"In fact, he shot all of the animals here. I shot a few as well, but they don't make the walls of fame. Hierarchy, you see..." He pointed at the sizeable head of a cape buffalo. "That was a superb shot. Three hundred yards with a Parker Hale point-four-one-six."

Lomu had never heard of the weapon. He was a soldier and used whatever tool he was given for the job. When he killed, it had been for Queen and country. Except for some dark days in what he referred to as his 'wilderness years' working as a mercenary. It hadn't always been that way. After he had been victim to savage and ill-conceived government cuts to the military, Lomu had worked on the private security circuit as a bodyguard. Here, the lines became blurred, but the paycheques still came in. Before he had known it, he had been a gun for hire for wealthy busi-nessmen and Third World governments. Not until a specialist department within Britain's own MI5 had hired a group of mercenaries for a deniable operation had Lomu emerged back into the light. And now? He did not know whether he was still welcome in the Security Service. He had been injured while on duty and simply dropped everything a few days ago to come and help at the request of his sister.

"Not a hunter?" Carter asked lightly. "It doesn't surprise me. Men aren't men anymore! The world is overrun by fucking snowflakes these days. Fucking vegans, fucking *Me Too*, fucking inclusivity..." He shook his head. "It's all fucked up..."

"My less than eloquent friend, though he has a gutter mouth and propensity to try and fit the F-word into every other sentence, has a valid point indeed..." the voice was rich and textured like a seasoned theatre actor who had just got his teeth into the leading role in Hamlet or Macbeth. "I'm McGregor," he announced pointedly, like it should mean something to whoever he introduced himself to.

Lomu saw the man who had been on the balcony now standing to his left. He hadn't made any sound as he had entered, and he wondered whether the lion and the cape buffalo had heard him either. Lomu suspected a resounding 'no' would be the answer. McGregor looked like a postcard for the tropics in the nineteen-thirties. As Lomu took in the man's Panama hat and colonial tropical dress, he thought the man's voice to be desperately at odds with his name. He shrugged, and said, "Fuck me, it's the man from Del Monte..." He paused, noting the indignation in McGregor's expression. "I always loved your pineapple juice..."

"Funny," the man said mirthlessly. "I actually own several pineapple plantations in Queensland as it goes. If you ever need employment, I'm always after some hardworking blacks come planting and picking time..."

Lomu took a step towards him, and Carter stepped between them, his hand on the handle of his knife.

"Easy, fella," he said. "It's the man's house, he can say what the fuck he likes."

"It's true," said McGregor. "About the blacks, that is. The Australian aborigines are the laziest, most bone-idle race on the planet. You just can't train them. Lab rats learn more quickly than Aborigines. Not like the Afro-Caribbean's. They can be trained all day long. Well, just look at several hundred years of the slave trade. We can't have been wrong." He smiled. "Am I touching a nerve, Davinder?"

Lomu took a breath, remembering what his father had once told him. *Start by counting off ten seconds silently. If you are still angry on nine, then punch on ten.* Nine out of ten times, he was able to control his considerable temper and rage, an important factor given both his size and strength. It was a quality that had kept him on the right side of the law his entire life. Well, mostly. He knew that McGregor was trying to needle him, so he ignored the racism, bigotry and preposterous nature of the man's opening salvo. But he wouldn't forget. It was all in the bank.

"No," Lomu replied. "I've met bigots all my life, and they're always compensating for something."

"Touché!" McGregor grinned. "Come, be my guest."

Lomu had to fight every instinct to refuse. McGregor was the last man he wanted to spend time with, Carter notwithstanding, but he was here out of his own curiosity as much as the veiled threat of the invite. He was led through a corridor, past row upon row of animal trophies with glass eyes and distant stares. Carter followed, but Lomu made sure he could see the man, either in his periphery as he surveyed the macabre zoo, or in the reflection of the glass, soulless eyes. They emerged in a second reception room with an ornate marble staircase which swept upwards in a half-spiral. The reception room reminded Lomu of grand halls he had seen in period dramas, even though he was not a fan of the genre and had never settled on one as he had channel surfed with the remote on one of the rare occasions when he watched television. As they headed out towards the sunlight of a distant sunroom, McGregor paused beside a vast desk with an old typewriter and several pens arranged in a fan on a blotter.

"Hemingway's," he said proudly. "I have read all his works. Are you familiar?"

His friend King had once lent him The Old Man and the Sea. A book his colleague had once read while taking some downtime in Cuba, the setting of for the book, and where Earnest Hemingway had written 'his masterpiece'. Lomu had thought it went on a bit. "I know who he is," he replied.

"Hemingway was a *real* man," McGregor announced approvingly. "A fan of the splendour of bullfights, of the nobility of pugilism, of rites of passage, of booze and gambling, of wine, woman and song!"

"I've heard that the man's writing wasn't up to much. That people revered his lifestyle more than his work, and that many of those same people only lusted after his lifestyle because they were inferior in the same aspects of their own lives. Compensating heavily." Lomu shrugged. "So, his following is largely made up of armchair adventurers, those who could never possibly emulate such a figure."

McGregor stared at him, then slowly reached for a rifle that was propped against a bookcase. He smiled as Lomu visibly tensed. "Hemingway was a superb writer. He was a master, because he only used three words when other writers of the day would use ten."

Lomu carried on unperturbed. "He knew his readers, I suppose. I guess he didn't want to put strain on them..."

McGregor stared long and hard, visibly insulted. "Hemingway shot the *Big Five* with this very rifle. That's the five most desired beasts to kill in Africa. I paid over one-hundred-thousand US dollars for this rifle. And I have killed every single one of the big five with it." He paused, working the bolt and aiming the rifle out of the doorway towards a swimming pool that glistened in the sunlight. "Do you know the skill involved in killing an African elephant, for example?"

Lomu shrugged. "Let me see... fuck all?" He smiled, enjoying the crestfallen expression upon McGregor's face. "The world's largest land animal with a rifle that I'm guessing has three times the power of a standard NATO infantry round. Yeah, fuck all skill would be my guess..."

"Five times the power of an assault rifle, actually. And I see that you are clearly ignorant in such matters of this wonderful sport. It takes skill to stalk the beast, skill to use a weapon with iron sights, not optics, and to get to within fifty yards of the most dangerous animal on the plains. And then the target is no bigger than a saucer. That is where the heart is but happens to be surrounded by the toughest hide in the animal kingdom and the largest and densest rib bones in nature."

"Well done," Lomu replied sardonically.

McGregor smiled. "Not a fan of hunting?" He nodded as if it was unexpected, but something he could accept.

"If I hunt, then it is for food. Not pleasure."

McGregor nodded, seemingly accepting the sentiment. He pointed to a curious piece hanging on the wall. "Then how about history and culture?" he asked, but he did not wait for a reply. "That is a Fijian weapon, found on an archaeological dig in the north of the island. It dates all the way back to the migration of Polynesia." He took it down from the wall and smiled as he handed it to his guest. It looked like a flat piece of driftwood that had been shaped into a makeshift bat with the one-dimensional profile of a cricket bat. The craftsman had then carved out a groove on the narrow edge all the way around on all but enough for a handle and had slotted teeth into the groove and bound each individual tooth tightly with thin, leather cordage. It was a frighteningly efficient-looking weapon. "Tiger shark teeth," McGregor announced somewhat proudly. Lomu already knew what type of teeth they had been, but in fairness, he had never seen them so large. "The tiger shark tooth has a saw edge, sharp enough to slice cleanly through a sheet of paper, and those teeth were taken from a tiger shark at least eighteen to twenty feet in length, according to Hawaii Institute of Marine Biology." He paused as much for effect as to draw breath. "What you have in your hands is a thousand-year-old chainsaw made solely for the purpose of war..." He paused. "It will hack through flesh and bone with considerable ease, as well as through other weapons." McGregor swept a hand towards the vast wall, every space filled with clubs and makeshift knives with flint blades, and spears. "Over there is the Aboriginal section from my home-land. Yes, I know it's hard to believe, but I spent many years in England and went to boarding school there, and obvi-ously went up to Oxford." He paused. "Believe it or not, those are all boomerangs..."

Lomu studied the selection of carved wooden pieces. Many looked like clubs, others were asymmetrical and vaguely boomerang shaped. There was nothing on the wall that looked remotely like the images one conjured up at the word. And certainly nothing that looked like it would ever come back once thrown.

"What about that one?" Lomu pointed at something that looked more like an Irish shillelagh. It was a long and thin curved club with a heavy-looking bulbous end that was carved and polished and covered in lacquer. The wood looked to have been burned, which indicated it had been fire-hardened.

"Yes, still a boomerang. Basically, a throwing club. That would take down a buffalo, except the *Abos* never had game that big until the Western settlers civilised the place. No, like the tiger shark saw, that is a weapon of war also."

"Have you ever been to war, McGregor?" Lomu looked past him, his eyes catching the glint from a curious half-moon sliver of metal hanging from a length of leather cordage.

The man shrugged. "Alas, no."

"Alas?" Lomu looked back at McGregor, unable to hide his contempt. "I have always found it intriguing that it's always the ones who talk about it that have never, nor *could* ever step up. Like the over-indulgent fans of Hemingway, I suppose. They love the idea of it more than the reality."

McGregor nodded sagely, then held up his hands. "I have dedicated my life to the pursuit of money and influence," he said. "I perhaps missed my calling. But that is the sacrifice I have made to be in the position I am today. I hunt and go fishing for game fish. Those are my outlets for aggression and primeval urges, which would otherwise have been satiated in the theatre of war."

Lomu shook his head. "That's not why men become soldiers. Not the vast majority, anyway." He paused. "Only the odd nutcase like you, for instance. A few sadly slip through."

"Why do you continue to try to antagonise me?" McGregor asked. "I invited you here for breakfast and a proposition."

Lomu dropped the Fijian shark-tooth club on the desk, scattering the late, great Ernest Hemingway's fountain pens and nudging the typewriter askew. "Okay then. Let's eat..."

TWELVE

McGregor put on a good spread. Or rather his kitchen did. The chef and maid brought out the platters and silently placed them on the table. Carter joined them, sitting in the middle of the large oval marble table, with Lomu and McGregor afforded the prominent positions at each end.

There were plates of fruit and pastries, sliced cold cuts and cheese. Scrambled eggs, bacon, sausages and grilled tomatoes arrived in a variety of warmed silver gastronome dishes, with racks of toast, although Lomu already knew that acceptable toast was an impossibility in the tropics. The humidity was no friend of a slice of toast.

Both McGregor and Carter ate too freely for the food to have been tampered with, so Lomu showed the two men what six-foot-four and eighteen stone of Fijian could do with such a spread. He washed down the food with glass after glass of freshly squeezed orange juice.

"You were on my land early this morning," McGregor said casually as he helped himself to more coffee.

Lomu sipped his own coffee. He had been told that it was an Indian blend from *Fortnum & Mason*, and that

McGregor had business interests in the region where the coffee beans were grown. The coffee was rich and full flavoured yet carried none of the tobacco overtones he associated with Colombian blends.

"I was wondering if you had buried the pickup trucks used in last night's hit and run at Kintoto Point," Lomu replied matter-of-factly. "People were killed and injured. A family also had their bure destroyed."

McGregor frowned while Carter remained impassive and Lomu wondered whether Carter ever showed any expression or emotion. He would certainly not enjoy playing the man at poker.

"I don't follow," McGregor said quietly.

"There was some trouble at the point. Drunk driver or something," Carter told him dismissively, like the tragedy was nothing. "Some of the boys were talking about it this morning. We have workers in both camps. Fortunately, they can see the future and know which side their bread is buttered."

"And you think vehicles from my development were involved?" McGregor asked incredulously.

Lomu nodded.

"Were the vehicles sign-written?" McGregor persisted.

Lomu shook his head.

"Then why would you think I or any of my associates were involved?"

"Because I think it's your style. Riding through the residents rough-shod, like it's the Wild West."

"That's a dangerous allegation," said Carter.

"You sent a couple of men after me yesterday. They had words with me at a fruit stand on the coast road."

"Did they tell you that I sent them?" McGregor asked casually.

Lomu thought about the fear in the man's eyes while his companion was out cold. He cursed himself for already saying too much. "Not in so many words," he replied. He had made his point, both with the two thugs and with McGregor. There was nothing to be gained from putting the two men at risk. "Just a feeling I got."

"And you're a fucking psychic, are you?" Carter scoffed. "I've heard enough of this crap!"

McGregor looked at him and shook his head. "Mr Lomu is my guest. Let's hear what he has to say..."

Carter bit down on a crusty bread roll, scowling at Lomu. His face had flushed red, and he was perspiring despite the air-conditioning and oscillating ceiling fan above them.

"I think you sent men into the village at Kintoto Point, and I think you have had the vehicles destroyed or hidden."

"Which?" asked McGregor. "First you trespass onto my land looking for the place I supposedly buried them, now you think I have had them destroyed." He paused. "You must make up your mind, my friend, because the first I heard of the incident was thirty seconds ago from your own lips."

"I know what you're up to. And I think Mustafa and Monique knew, too."

McGregor shook his head in protest. "I have millions invested, sunken even, into that project. The families were all financially compensated and agreed to move."

Lomu frowned. It was the first he had heard about a pay-out, and he cursed both Marie and Delilah for not giving him all the facts. It didn't change matters regarding Mustafa and Monique, but it certainly added to the overall picture.

"Their bullshit claims about Kintoto Point being sacred

land has cost us tens of thousands of dollars a day in stop-pages," Carter said vehemently.

"Us?"

"The company."

McGregor nodded. "Close to a million a week in labour, permits, equipment and plant hire, and insurances." He paused. "We are keen to get back to work, I'm sure you can understand that?"

Lomu had no choice but to nod, and the moment he did, he felt he had lost a crucial battle. McGregor seemed to realise this too and smiled. Lomu sipped some more coffee, watching the two men like a mongoose watches a pair of snakes. Warily, and waiting for them to make the next move.

"Are you a wolf or a sheep, Mr Lomu?" McGregor asked eventually.

"Nah, he's a sheepdog," Carter interjected. "He likes to look after the sheep and chase off the wolves..." He sneered. "Isn't that right?"

Lomu said nothing.

"But with enough wolves, the sheepdog doesn't stand a chance," said McGregor. "And nor do the sheep."

"Poor little sheep..." Carter grinned.

McGregor smiled. "Sheep spend their lives fearing the wolf. The shepherd keeps the sheep safe, but only with the aid of the sheepdog." He paused, lighting a fat Cuban cigar as he still chewed his bacon. "But it's the shepherd who kills and eats the sheep in the end. Not the wolves. And when this happens, the sheepdog isn't even in the equation. The sooner you work this out, the sooner you will understand life and the order to it..."

"And you're the shepherd, I suppose?"

"Exactly," McGregor replied. He looked at Carter, then

back at Lomu. "We both are. We control the sheep and have our sheepdogs scare off the wolves." He paused. "It's time not to decide whether you're a wolf, a sheep or a sheepdog, but whether you are a shepherd. If you are, then we can help you. Financially. You left and turned your back on your people for twenty-years. With enough money in your bank account, I can virtually guarantee that you will not think about this little speck in the Pacific again."

And there it was. Lomu hadn't thought about home much over the years. He had left under his own ideas of right and wrong, and he had turned his back on his family to the same degree that they had turned on him. He had drawn a line under his former life, preferring to live with the memories of a happy childhood and idolising the father he remembered so fondly; not of Josefa taking his father's place, nor of the way everyone had so seamlessly accepted the way his mother had moved on. The rage had fired him through life, spurred him onto greater things. He had been the youngest corporal in the British army, the youngest solider to earn the Distinguished Service Medal and the youngest recipient of the George Cross. Upon getting 'badged' in the SAS, he soon earned a reputation as a fierce friend and loyal team member. Being considerably larger than most SAS troopers, who were typically wiry, strong and referred to by the regular army as 'racing snakes', he was most people's first choice on the team, often for his loadbearing ability, but mainly for his unflappable nature and voice of reason. And his loyalty. He looked at McGregor and said, "I can't be bought."

"Only because nobody has tried yet."

Lomu had been tested before after a massacre in Burkina Faso. He had given evidence against the notorious and reprehensible Russian security outfit, The Wagner

Group. He had refused to be bought off, and when three of their 'security consultants' had visited him in the dead of night, he had left them to be collected in body bags. Even now, Wagner contractors could earn two million US dollars on an open contract for *Name: Lomu (first name unknown), Sex: Male, Ethnicity: Black, Place of Birth: Unknown (possibly Caribbean), Height: 193cm, Weight: 114.3kg, Additional: former British army.*

"People have tried," he replied, getting up from his seat.

"Maybe they never offered you enough money?" Carter ventured. He looked at McGregor quite seriously and said, "How smoothly do we want this to go?"

"Smoothly," McGregor replied. "I've had enough of pissing about." He looked back at Lomu and said, "Two hundred and fifty thousand pounds. Just to get on a plane today. Don't be a fool, walk away."

Lomu smiled. "Oh, I'll certainly be walking away," he said. "But I'm not getting on a plane anytime soon."

"Three hundred," McGregor said quickly. "Two minutes and the press of a button and it's in your account."

"There's a missing girl," Lomu said measuredly. "And she is my half-sister."

"You never even knew you had a sister until yesterday," Carter interjected.

"We know nothing about a missing girl, other than the fact that there is one. Nobody from McGregor Enterprises is responsible for a missing girl, nor the sad fate of a young man." McGregor shook his head. "The accusation is ridiculous."

Lomu stared at McGregor, then at Carter, trying to read the man's expression. Carter seemed a closed book, while McGregor protested emphatically. The truth, he wouldn't know how to read either man in a game of poker.

"Very well, Mr Lomu. Half a million pounds, but you're on a flight out of here... anywhere... today." McGregor paused. "I can't afford further delays, nor god forbid, the project to become derailed. Five hundred thousand pounds and you simply fly anywhere and forget about a few huts on a beach, and a family who you haven't seen in twenty years." He shrugged. "You already forget about Kintoto Point once before, you can forget about it again."

Lomu's father had once told him that every man would eventually face a decision between what was right, and what was easy. The man you became depended on which decision you took. Easy decisions were always harder to live with given the passage of time. He shook his head and headed out through the pool and patio area. Behind him, Carter jeered but McGregor remained silent. As he crossed the terracotta-coloured pavers and walked down the driveway, he had the uneasy feeling that he was being watched. Which indeed he was.

THIRTEEN

Lomu had rounded the first bend and was clear of the house when he saw the car. It was a light blue Holden, and he was reminded of the country's trading deal with Australia. Holden was now defunct but was once owned by General Motors and basically a Vauxhall made in Australia, but often with more interesting engines. Australia was a country in which you could build a lot of miles and risk overheating, so larger engine blocks from the US had found a place there. This one sounded like it had a V8 under the bonnet and warbled a throaty baritone note, that echoed off the mountainside. As it drew nearer, Lomu could see Shabnam in the passenger seat and the white officer she had been with yesterday was behind the steering wheel.

The vehicle pulled over and Shabnam got out, tucking her white silk blouse into her trousers as she walked towards him. "Find anything?"

"Nope."

"You searched all over?"

"Yep."

"So, that wasn't enough, and you went to the man's

house?" she asked, unable to hide her surprise. "Nothing subtle about that."

"I got invited to breakfast."

"And?"

"I had bacon and eggs."

"That's it?"

"I had coffee and orange juice as well." He paused. "The coffee was from Fortnum and Mason's and the juice was freshly squeezed."

"You know what I mean."

"I was intrigued. They made the invite a little on the compulsory side, so rather than fight it out I went along to see what made the man tick."

"And what did you discover?"

"He thrives on power. Money and influence are everything to him, as is his ego."

"I could have told you that," she replied dismissively. "What else did you find out?"

Lomu nodded. "I got to know enough," he said quietly. "Anyway, you're not going to get anywhere with those trucks. They both maintain that they know nothing about it. Besides, McGregor delighted in asking me if the vehicles were sign-written. Those trucks are long-gone. You're not going to find them."

"So, you've got nothing..." she stated flatly.

"I wouldn't say that," he replied.

"Where are you going now?"

"Back to Kintoto to get my car."

"Hang around and I'll give you a lift."

Lomu shook his head. "Go do your job. If I see you, I'll see you." He carried on walking with the sun now burning down on his back. He turned and watched the Holden continue up the drive, its V8 rumbling and sounding in need of a heavy right foot to lift the note. He'd never owned a fast car, but McGregor's offer would have changed that, but you can't miss what you've never had. He carried on walking, setting a good pace, with Shabnam's words echoing in his mind. *"So, you've got nothing..."* Well, he wouldn't have said that. He had counted the CCTV cameras, noticed the deactivated pressure mats in doorways and could recall the entire ground floor layout from memory. He had made a note of the alarm system and the alarm control panel in the entrance hall. "No, not *nothing*," he said to himself. "A first-class reconnaissance is what I got, luv..."

FOURTEEN

The mountain road was steep and winding, but by traversing the grassy terraces between the hairpin bends, he shaved hundreds of metres off every section. Only when he reached a sheer slope of rock did he continue along the road. Hearing a rumbling engine, he turned, and half expected to see Shabnam and her driver in the Holden, deciding he might as well accept the lift and get on with what he had planned next.

It wasn't the Holden. Instead, a large and battered American truck trundled towards him. He did not know the make, but he was sure that it was from the seventies and from the sound of it, a large V8 nestled in the expansive engine bay. The truck was rusted with what purists called a 'patina' where layers and layers of paint added over the years had worn down in places to a layer of smooth rust that gave the vehicle a dystopian look. Either that, or it was just an old jalopy that wouldn't die.

Lomu moved onto the verge and carried on walking. Right up until the driver floored the accelerator and the vehicle's rear wheels lit up on the tarmac like a drag racer on an American quarter mile strip. Lomu turned just in time to see the truck hurtling towards him. He dived out of the way but fell off the rocky precipice and landed heavily in the brush ten feet below the road. The bushes broke the worst of his fall, but not his momentum, and he slid through the undergrowth for thirty feet or so, then free-fell eight feet to the road below. Parachute trained and the veteran of at least a thousand jumps, it did nothing for him and he landed in a crumpled heap having not had the time nor instinct to aid his landing. The wind was knocked from his lungs, and he took several precious seconds to get his bearings, but the sound of the thunderous V8 told him that the driver was intent on killing him, and that he was rounding the hairpin bend in the distance, hellbent on mowing him down. He got unsteadily to his feet and limped across the road to the verge, where thankfully the slope was more gradual, and the grass was short. He placed his hands on the low barrier and hopped painfully over. There was nothing else for it, so he dropped onto his left side and slid the fifty metres or so to the next section of road below, the vehicle pausing just above him before tearing off in a cacophony of mechanical protest, and a squeal of smoking tyres. When he stopped sliding, he was lying on his back in a gulley of shale and gravel. All around him were rocks the size of pavers and he grabbed up two of them, one in each hand, and got unsteadily to his feet. He could not see the truck, but he could hear it, and he knew that he had enough time to confuse the driver. Dropping the rocks, he stripped off his shirt and tossed it into the middle of the road. Picking up the two heavy rocks, he ran up the road towards the sound of the approaching truck, crossed over and stood next to a large eucalyptus tree, its trunk substantially wide enough to conceal even his massive frame. The truck's engine resonated, its rear wheels spinning as the driver drifted it skilfully through the bend and accelerated up through the gears. Suitably, the driver slowed when he saw Lomu's shirt in the road ahead, but it was already too late. Lomu stepped out and hurled the rock at the windscreen. He passed the second rock to his right hand as the first rock shattered the windscreen, and he pitched the second rock with all his might. The rock travelled in a slight arc, through the open window and into the driver's shocked face. Lomu saw the man slump in his seat as the vehicle veered across the road and into the barrier. The large truck, with its oversized all-terrain tyres made short work of the barrier and took off into the air as if it had hit a ramp. The wheels spun freely, the engine suddenly hitting maximum revs as the vehicle went airborne and disappeared. Lomu heard the ear-splitting sound of metal on asphalt a full five seconds later, and then the sound of trees snapping and splitting and rocks dislodging and of metal crunching as the truck rolled through the undergrowth and pitched over the edge of the next section of road and off the cliff. He did not hear the vehicle meet the water two hundred feet below, just the sound of Shabnam's warbling V8 as he picked up his shirt and turned around to see the Holden driving out of the bend. He smiled, held out his thumb and waited for his lift.

FIFTEEN

"I can't see anything down there," Shabnam said as she cupped her hand against the sun and stared down into the ocean. "I'll have to get a search team out here immediately."

"Unless..."

"Unless, what?"

Lomu shrugged. "We use it to unsettle McGregor."

"How?"

Lomu did not take his eyes off the water. It was deep blue and looked slick, mesmerising in the sunlight as it ebbed and flowed, washing surf on the foot of the cliff. "They sent this guy to kill me..."

"It could have just been a robbery, an opportunist," she ventured. "Either way, there's a vehicle down there and a body. The tourist commission don't like bodies washing up on the beaches, and nobody likes a law enforcement officer who doesn't report a crime or incident when they're aware of one. Even if it's a roadside robber, or whatever else his intention, like the man down there."

He looked at her and smiled. "I highly doubt that luv." He paused, grinning at her expression. It was clear that nobody had ever called her 'luv' before. He could picture her career; working twice as hard as the men she served with, fiercely independent, first on the scene, last to leave. She wasn't one to have hitched a ride on her way up the ranks. "No, this guy wanted me dead, that was what he had been hired, or ordered, to do. They knew that I was walking back. They offered me five-hundred thousand pounds to leave. This guy could have done it for a couple of thousand."

"A few hundred, even," Shabnam interjected. "You'd be surprised how little people earn on Fiji."

He nodded. He'd already bought-off a porter to look the other way with little more than a hundred pounds. "But now their guy has disappeared, and I'm still alive. Just like when I stopped for something to eat yesterday, and two guys tried to jump me."

"Somebody attacked you yesterday?"

"They tried."

"And they're dead as well?"

"No. Just a couple of fat lips, that's all." He held up his hands in mock surrender. "I promise..."

"Who were they?"

He shrugged. "A couple of fishermen in a white Mitsubishi pickup. One of them confessed to being paid to do me over." She frowned and he added, "Beaten up."

She nodded. "So, they've progressed from sending men to give you a beating to sending them to kill you in just one day? This isn't good..."

"Well, technically, somebody could have been trying to kill me last night at the cook-out," he replied. "I find it difficult to believe I wasn't the target. The entire feast was put on for me."

"And you still think you weren't missed for twenty years?"

He shrugged. "Well, when you put it like that."

"Brothers," she stated flatly. "I've got one just like you. The world revolves around brothers, while the world turns because of sisters."

"You and Marie should go for a drink," he replied dryly. "You'd have a great deal in common to talk about."

She smiled. "No, I won't be having a drink with Marie anytime soon." She paused, exhaling a breath so deep that she was clearly unburdening pent-up emotion. "People like me have sold out in the eyes of people like Marie," she said coolly.

"Meaning?"

Shabnam shrugged. "Meaning that I work for the police and the police do what the government says. Or at least that's how people like her see it. We have our own remit, and it's to serve the civilian population. There have been several government overthrows and coups in recent years, but I believe the police have kept to that remit, even with the military trying to enforce martial law." She paused. "But Marie, her husband Jake and a few at the Point have become more and more militant in trying to keep their way of life and stop any new developments in the area. They've taken on developers before, but now that they have crossed swords with McGregor, it's not working out so well for them."

"Do you know Marie's husband?" Lomu asked.

"His name is Jake. Yeah, I know him."

"I believe he works away. A roughneck, or oil rig worker I should say."

She scoffed, then her expression softened when she

realised Lomu was being serious. "No, he's in jail. He had a series of run-ins with McGregor's construction crew, then set fire to a load of their equipment. Diggers, bulldozers and earth movers. A million US dollars' worth. Most of it was hired, and because it was in a compound, uninsured. It cost McGregor not only a million, but he was refused hire from other companies and had to purchase more equipment. Jake has recently been sentenced to six years for arson. Most likely he'll be out in three if he's a good boy inside. I guess that's why Marie called you. She needed to finish what she started, and the death of Mustafa and disappearance of Monique was too much for her to deal with alone." Lomu nodded sagely. He had thought he had been needed, top of the list. But he had been the next best thing. A necessity. A piece on a chessboard. He had been painted a picture of big business swatting away the little person, but that little person had set fire to private property. "How deep do you think it is under the cliff?" she asked, looking down into the depths.

"I used to collect mussels and clams down there. It's at least eighty feet deep on the lowest tides of the year. Nobody is going to find that pickup truck in a hurry." She nodded, but she did not seem convinced, and certainly wasn't comfortable with her decision to delay calling it in. "How did you get on with McGregor and his stooge?" he asked, trying to distract her from listening to her conscience.

"As well as can be expected." She shrugged. "McGregor has public officials and high-ranking police officers on his payroll. He didn't give me anything, and if he did it wouldn't have gone much further. Not until I can find out who he specifically has in his pocket," she said adamantly. "He laughed me out of there. No signwriting on the two trucks, none of the drivers identified. Nothing."

"I shot one of them with a shotgun. Have you tried the hospitals?"

She nodded. "It's not that easy. Fiji is awash with private clinics, private ambulance services, even. We have tried the main hospitals and clinics and so far, haven't turned up anything." She paused. "Technically I should arrest you for discharging a weapon unlawfully."

"It was self-defence."

"You'll probably find a lot of countries still don't allow its citizens to go around shooting each other. Britain being one of them, and Fiji being another. There are few countries like the United States of America, thank goodness."

"Unless your life is in danger..." Lomu mused. He had always agreed with the doctrine that it was better to be tried by twelve than carried by six. Nobody was ever going to tell him that he couldn't defend himself with whatever he had to hand.

"If McGregor is behind this..."

"He is," Lomu interrupted.

"*If* he is, then you run the risk of antagonising him further. You may not be so lucky next time."

"It's what you want, isn't it?"

"A stalking horse and a head above the parapet all at once." Shabnam frowned and he explained. "In warfare to draw fire from the enemy, usually a sniper, someone occasionally has to risk sticking their head up briefly for the sniper to take a shot. Hopefully, they get their head down in time, but the sniper draws attention to his position. It's chancy, but it works. I'm sticking my head out for McGregor. Hopefully he'll show his hand and incriminate himself."

"And a stalking horse, what is that?"

"It was a fake horse, either a cut-out or made from

wicker, that hunters hid behind and worked their way closer to whatever they were trying to shoot. I'm the stalking horse and you're the hunter. With McGregor's eye on me, maybe he won't see you coming..."

"Maybe."

"I still don't know who to trust," she said.

"Then don't trust anybody."

"Except you?"

"You came to me, remember?" He stepped away from the edge of the precipice and looked at her. She was around five-feet-six, and no more than nine stone. Athletic and lithe. She would have had to train and fight hard to outdo her colleagues and rise to the top. He imagined she could run and keep running, fight and keep fighting. Like an infantry soldier. But she would have had to be sharp, intelligent as well. She was attractive, and that would have been a hinderance. Positive discrimination. Her shoulder length hair was jet black and pulled back in a simple ponytail, and he found himself wanting to see what she looked like when she let it down. He wanted to see more of her than that, too.

"I did," she agreed. "Because you couldn't possibly be on McGregor's payroll, and you have a vested interest in finding the girl."

"Her name is Monique," he told her.

"I'm sorry."

"Don't sweat it." He shrugged. "I didn't even know I had a half-sister until four days ago."

She punched his arm playfully. "Damn you!" She laughed. "You had me feeling bad for not using her name, but I know her better than you do!"

Lomu nodded. "But you don't have much to do with anyone on the Point now?"

"No, not really. I represent officialdom, I guess."

Lomu said nothing. In the distance he could see the island of Uluwala, the small, inhabited island where both Mustafa and Monique had gone in their quest to prove that Kintoto Point was indeed sacred land. He could see the distant island, no more than a haze in the distance, but he had no idea what to look for if he went there. He supposed finding a boat would be a start. He had only been there once before, but he remembered he hadn't liked it. The people there prided themselves on being descendants of Christian missionaries. He had felt that they had looked down on him, despite the fact he had been raised with a broad array Christian, Fijian folklore and Muslim teachings. In short, the Lomu clan had been taught right from wrong and brought up in an honest and charitable environment. But the people of Uluwala had seemed judgemental, supercilious and indifferent. He supposed he would see how much the island had changed, but first he needed to get a ride back to Kintoto Point and collect his vehicle. He also needed to dress a few new wounds – cuts and grazes - and check on his shoulder, which had started to seep at one of the sutures. He guessed a shower and a change of clothes would be on that list, too.

"Well, I'll let officialdom drop me short of the village," Lomu told her. "I wouldn't want to be tarred with the same brush."

"So, I'm cramping your style?" She paused. "Maybe you should walk?"

"No, I've wasted enough time already."

SIXTEEN

Lomo could see Marie getting into her battered Suzuki Jeep when he walked into the camp, having been dropped off by Shabnam further up the beach near one of the proposed entrances to the development. He had wanted to jog down the deserted strip of sand to clear his head, but everything ached from the fall and the grazes had started to clot and pulled and tore open as he walked. Perspiration ran down his legs and stung the scratches, cuts and grazes, and although he had lived in Fiji for his first sixteen years and served and trained in plenty of hot countries over the years, he was finding it difficult to acclimatise. He held up a hand as Marie drove by and she stopped and wound down her window, a blast of air-conditioning hitting him in the face, providing him with some relief. She must have been out already or left the engine running for the cold air to be running so efficiently.

"You missed breakfast," she said tartly.

Lomu could see some plates of cling-wrapped food on the passenger seat. "You were coming to find me with my breakfast?"

She scoffed loudly. "You've been gone for twenty years and still you think the world revolves around you..." She glanced at the food, then back at her brother. "No, this is some of the food from last night. I know an old couple who will be most grateful for whatever I can spare."

"Oh..." he replied lamely. He was about to mention her husband and his 'oil worker' job but thought better of it. There was an edge to her mood today, quite understandable in light of last night's attack on the beach, and he thought better of it. She must have been embarrassed that her husband was in prison, which just went to show what a gulf lay between the two siblings. There was so much he had missed; how could he have ever expected her to confide in him? "Well, from what I ate, it was delicious, I'm sure they'll appreciate it. Any news on the casualties?"

"Wow, now that's down to business..." she said acidly. "Four people injured, and Sarah Afihah died. Remember her? She was Tipi's mom, only Tipi drowned on a fishing trip. You were great friends with him growing up. Ever get in contact with him over the years? He died about eight years ago..." She paused, letting the news sink in somewhat cruelly. "Anyway, I thought you'd know everything about everything hanging out with that bitch Shabnam."

He looked at her and said, "You don't get on with her?"

"Like I said, she's a bitch, Davinder. And she's not to be trusted. She must have stepped on a lot of people to get where she is in her fancy career..." She pulled away without another word, the tiny Suzuki spraying sand on his stinging legs. Lomu watched her go, puzzled by her reaction. What more could he do? He had dropped everything to be here; discharged himself from hospital and left his team at MI5 high and dry after their most recent mission. He knew that both King and Caroline would be going after one of the escaped killers they had been up against, and he knew that they could do with all the help they could get with that. He wondered whether it was simply too late in being here. Mustafa had been killed and Monique was missing. Everyone suspected what was meant by that – they simply hadn't found her body yet. It had been good to see his mother again, but he knew it was different now. She had moved on, too. Everybody had. So why the hell was he still here trying to find a girl he had never met, who statistically was already dead, and save a way of life he had not been a part of for twenty years? Things changed. It was the same the world over. Villages became towns and towns became cities. People woke up every day and realised that their rural bliss was being advanced upon by suburbia and developments. Why should a few people living in huts be any different? Shabnam had seen the writing on the wall and got out to build herself a career, and Delilah kept a foot in both camps as she earned money in the city, kept an apartment and visited her family at Kintoto Point. But for how long? Those trips out here would become less frequent, and once the development went through and the villagers moved on, he doubted she would even look back. That's how life worked. You simply couldn't go home again. Never go back.

He cursed himself coming here; cursed himself for staying away for so long. But most of all, he simply cursed all the way over to the bure where he found his bag packed on the sofa bed, which had been turned back into a sofa. He unzipped it and took out his washbag and headed into the tiny bathroom. He ran a shower while he shaved and brushed his teeth with his travel toothbrush, then got under the spray and soaped, shampooed and hissed through his teeth as the soap stung his cuts, but the hot water soon helped his bruises and he relaxed for the first time since his dawn swim. He checked his watch. It was almost eleven and too much of the day had been wasted. He adjusted the spray down to as cold as it would go and stood there for a few minutes before getting out. By the time he dried off and picked out his clean clothes, he was perspiring once more. He settled on cargoes and a T-shirt and having learned his lesson from travelling without socks on the plane, put on a pair of thin tennis socks before slipping on some lightweight walking shoes with a decent tread. He looked at the shotgun hanging on the wall and shrugged like he was in enough trouble already, and took it down, checking the breech. He found the cartridges in the dresser and took the remainder of the box. He inspected the box closely. 12-gauge, 32g, No.5 shot. He hadn't used many shotguns in his military career, other than a Remington pump-action loaded with the Hatton Round, a load designed to breach door locks and hinges during an armed assault. But he did know that these cartridges were a general-purpose load good for small game, birds in flight and close-up, would drop a bull. He remembered many of the local fishermen had used single barrelled shotguns as harpoon launchers when he was young. A harpoon with a tube welded on the end would sleeve over the barrel and when used with a 12-bore blank cartridge – often the fishermen would simply empty out the shot, remove the wad and cut down and re-crimp the cartridge – would tackle large tiger sharks or occasionally whales. He remembered when the entire village had feasted on whale meat each autumn. Migrating Minke whales were once prized not only for their meat and the oil that could fuel hurricane lanterns for most of the year, but also because they were manageable to hunt in small boats. Whale hunting around Fiji was outlawed now, like many of the cultural practices Fijian islanders had once needed to survive, and he knew that there was no need to continue a practice just because it used to be considered normal. There was now an abundance of supermarkets all over the island. Besides, if society continued age-old practices without change, then slavery would never have been abolished and women would not have the vote.

Lomu dropped his bag on the backseat of the hire vehicle and stowed the shotgun across the rear footwell. He fished a towel out of his bag and covered the weapon, then dropped the box of shells in the driver's door pocket. He hoped he would not need the shotgun, but Carter had already brandished a pistol and McGregor had at least one hunting rifle that he had seen. The truth was outside of farmers and fishermen who needed a firearm as a tool, not many people owned just one gun. If McGregor paid a fortune for a rifle with the kind of provenance he had enjoyed bragging about, then he would undoubtedly have others. Fiji's gun laws were among the strictest in the world and collectors needed special permits, while handguns and military style 'black rifles' were banned to civilians without special collector's permits or government permission. So, where did Carter get his pistol from? The answer was simple. Illegally purchased or smuggled into the country and illegally held, which meant that it would not be on any firearms register, and he would not fear using it, as he could simply dump it in the ocean if he ever fired it in anger.

Lomu glanced at the boats that had been pulled up on the sand. Wooden canoes, small wooden work boats and an aluminium dory. Nothing with an engine over 35 HP. Not the kind of craft he wanted to use to get to Uluwala. It would take him all day, and the ocean was a big and vulnerable place when you were in a small boat. His best option was to try and hire something more suitable at the harbour outside Suva.

The drive to Suva took him past stretches of icing sugar sand and clear shallow water, darkening steadily to the horizon to the deepest blue. Palm trees fringed the beaches and the straw roofed bures he remembered as a child were now bars and restaurants catering for pink coloured tourists rapidly burning in the sun. Bypassing the coast road, he climbed into the mountains where the air was cooler and he caught sight of cruise ships far out to sea and multiple small craft skipping across the clear water, foaming wake trailing far behind. He shook his head, wondering why he ever left. And then he remembered, a sear of pain somewhere inde-terminable inside that he had not felt so raw in years, as he remembered Josefa walking down the steps to the family bure, tears streaming as he hugged him close and told him that his father had passed. Cancer. His father had spared them all from knowing and only his mother and Josefa had known. He remembered both he and Marie thought he had been lain up with a bad back. And now, his mother was living through the cancer nightmare again with Josefa. He sighed loudly. He had been too slow to put his own feelings aside, too caught up in the fact that his mother and Josefa had moved on too quickly, and he had failed to empathise with either of them. Death affected everybody differently. A laugh was sometimes the only thing to stop someone from weeping, and a fond memory shared was sometimes all that kept a person from crumbling from grief.

Lomu started the descent and pulled off to the lesser used coast road. He found a layby, which was more of a strip of desolate ground, littered with food wrappers and plastic bottles and surrounded on three sides by waist-high weeds and grass. He switched off the engine, taking in the stillness. High above him, the main road hummed with traffic heading in and out of the city. He got out and took out his mobile phone, noted the messages, but discarded them without reading. Three from Rashid, two from Caroline, one from Flymo and nothing from King. Eleven from Ramsay. He smiled. Three, two and one from genuine concern, none because King would simply let Lomu get on with whatever he was doing and if he needed him, then he could ask. And then there were eleven types of bollocking he could do without. He dialled Ramsay's number and waited.

"What time do you call this?"

"Lunchtime."

"It's one in the morning..."

"Would you prefer I ring back?"

"No." Ramsay yawned. *"What in the name of all who's holy are you doing out there?"*

"I'm on holiday."

"I noticed. The service isn't picking up the tab for hire cars. Not unless you're on assignment, which you're not."

"Ramsay, just listen to me. I need you to look up somebody for me."

"Who?" Ramsay replied tersely.

"Well, a man *and* a company."

"What are you doing in Fiji?"

"Can you look this up for me?"

"I can look up anybody on earth," he replied matter-of-factly. *"Whether I decide to or not depends on you telling me what you are doing."*

"Family business."

"That's not enough, Dave."

"A boy has been killed and a girl is missing. I know this

man is behind it. The missing girl is my half-sister." He paused. "How's that?"

"*Better...*" Ramsay replied. "*Simon Mereweather wants to know whether you're coming back.*"

"Undecided."

"*Well, you don't just get to leave, Dave. There are protocols involved, papers to sign, veiled threats to be made, that sort of thing...*"

"You know where I am."

"*Quite.*"

"So, can you help?"

There was a pause and Lomu knew that he'd been put on hold. Ramsay came back on the line, and he wondered whether the MI5 chief operations officer had possibly got Simon Mereweather, the Director General of the Security Service on conference call. But he didn't care. They knew where he was, and he needed their help. The late hour was most likely his saving grace. One didn't wake up Director Generals at 1 AM unless Russia was about to press the button.

"Am I being recorded?"

"*No.*"

"Can the boss hear me?"

"*No.*" Ramsay paused. "*I'll keep this on the low down...*"

"The down low..." Lomu corrected him.

"*You're as bad as my teenaged daughter...*" He paused and Lomu could hear Ramsay writing something down. "*Alright, let me know who you're interested in. I have a pen and can just about see the page through bleary eyes now...*"

"His name is McGregor. First name unknown. He's fifty-five, at a guess. Australian, but educated at a public school in England, and he also mentioned that he was at Oxford. He owns pineapple plantations in Queensland and is undertaking a massive hotel and spa complex at Kintoto Point in Fiji. I suspect he has many business interests. He owns a property on Suva Drive, just north of the capital."

"Is that it?"

"You've worked miracles from less..."

"Company name?"

"McGregor Enterprises."

"Is that everything?"

"Not quite. Try Dan Carter. Forties, male, heavy Australian accent. He's a tough looking bloke. I get the impression he's been with McGregor for a while, most likely as his muscle. Without generalising, he looks a bit like Crocodile Dundee."

"Who?"

"The film with Paul Hogan."

"You want me to run a check on this Paul Hogan as well?"

"No, he's an actor."

"Carter?"

Lomu cursed under his breath. "No, Paul Hogan is an actor who played a part in a film called Crocodile Dundee. This guy Carter looks a bit like him, even dresses a bit like him, even down to the knife."

"Knife?"

"Bloody hell, Neil. You seriously haven't seen, or even *heard* of Crocodile Dundee? Just find a bloody clip to watch on *YouTube* and you'll get an idea of what sort of man this Carter is. As for McGregor, he's a fan of Ernest Hemingway, the writer. And I guess looks a bit like him, too. Greying, tidy beard, a little overweight. He said he bought a point-four-one-six African game rifle that belonged to Hemingway for over a hundred grand, and he owned a typewriter and some fountain pens that once belonged to

Hemingway, too. I imagine there will be a record of that, most likely an auction of some kind. Given the writer's status, one of the large auction houses like Sotheby's or Bonham's would be my guess."

"What the hell have you got yourself into, Dave?"

Lomu wanted to reply: *a whole lot of trouble,* but he didn't answer. Neil Ramsay was a solid character, but since they had all worked closely with him the team had realised that he was in fact, a highly functioning autistic. He was a fantastic planner because of this and could see the picture several moves ahead. He also had an encyclopaedic memory and an eye for detail. The downsides were that he seldom seemed in on the joke and had little in the way of diplomacy. Subtlety wasn't exactly his thing, either. Instead, Lomu said, "Nothing I can't handle, Neil." He paused, noticing a black Jeep Cherokee crawling slowly towards him on the dust road. Tourists, perhaps edging closer to the cliff for a photograph. Or a selfie. Did people even take landscape pictures anymore? He wondered. He watched the vehicle crawling forwards and realised that he had to have eyes in the back of his head. In truth, he had never worked alone more than a couple of times. "What are the team up to?" he asked, his eyes still on the Jeep.

Ramsay hesitated, then said, *"King and Caroline have gone after Natasha. They're not going to rest until the woman's dead. It's personal. We can't sanction that, and nor should we. Until then, I suppose they're on a sabbatical..."* He paused. *"We seem to have had a few more of those over the years. More than we ever should have. Frankly, I don't want to know what they have planned, I struggle with my conscience when I hear something incriminating..."*

"And Rashid?"

"I can't tell you that," Ramsay replied. *"He's going*

undercover. An infiltration assignment. I can't risk his security."

"No worries..."

"So, do we put this little escapade down as a sabbatical?"

"For now," Lomu replied. The Jeep was closer to him now. The windows were tinted and rolled up. Maybe the tourists wanted to use the air-conditioning more effectively. But their photography would be hampered by the tint. He was feeling uneasy. Something about the continuous approach. Like a cheetah starting its slow stalk before exploding towards a lightning attack. "Listen, Neil, thanks, I owe you." He ended the call. The Jeep crawled closer, the window cracking open a few inches. Lomu walked back to the truck. The shotgun rested tantalisingly close. He looked back at the Jeep. Still the vehicle crawled closer, the window lowering a fraction more. "Fuck it," he said, snatching up the shotgun. "Let's see what you've got..."

SEVENTEEN

Lomu had the shotgun aimed at the Jeep, three shells clutched in his giant left hand as he clutched the fore-end and brought the weapon to bear. The window lowered and Lomu fired. Nobody lowered a window when a gun was on them unless they were planning on shooting back. The glass shattered into a million tiny fragments and the vehicle lurched forwards and started to turn. Lomu broke the weapon and pulled out the spent shell case, slamming another into the breech and snapping the barrel closed. By the time he cocked the hammer back, gunshots sounded, and he saw the muzzle flashes inside the Jeep as the driver fired over his injured companion and attempted to steer with one hand, his eyes on Lomu as the vehicle turned a tight circle.

Despite the tinted windows, Lomu could see movement in the rear of the vehicle and as he aimed at the driver, the rear window smashed outwards and muzzle flashes lit up the inside of the car. Bullets fizzed past his ear and slammed into the dirt at his feet as two guns opened fire on him and left him feeling terribly exposed. Lomu sprinted back for the hire car as bullets peppered the rear passenger door. He ducked behind the rear of the vehicle as more bullets impacted against the rear quarter panel. He turned and fired, reloaded and fired again. This time, the passenger caught the full force of the blast and slumped still. The driver panicked and accelerated too hard, the Jeep already on a tight circle, its rear wheels digging into the dirt and slewing it sideways before the front driven wheels could counter. The big SUV drifted sideways and flattened the weeds and long grass, then disappeared. Lomu heard the screaming engine revs followed by an immeasurable silence as the vehicle went off the edge of the cliff and crashed into the rocks below, landing as loudly as cannon fire as the metal crumpled on the black volcanic rock. Lomu got to his feet and walked across the open ground towards the edge. He heard the 'woof' as the fuel ignited and walked no further as the mushroom-shaped cloud billowed upwards in front of him and dispersed a hundred feet above his head. Black, acrid smoke channelled in a pyre. As the fire raged and the smoke climbed steadily, Lomu risked a peek over the edge. There was nothing down there except for the burning hulk of a vehicle. The paint had already melted off the bodywork, such was the ferocity of the heat. Nobody had made it out. He could see along the entire slab of rock and other than washed-up flotsam and jetsam strewn along the hightide mark, the burning vehicle was the only other thing down there. He walked back to the car and stowed the shotgun back in the footwell, leaving a live shell in the breech, but un-cocked.

He drove on another mile and stopped at a filling station with a mini mart. It was a *Superfresh*, part of a chain throughout the island. Lomu didn't need fuel, but he could do with some water, and it was about time for first lunch. Or second breakfast. He was jet-lagged, after all. The market was cool, both air-conditioning and oscillating fans doing a superb job. He selected a tuna wrap, some crisps and a six-pack of individual bottled water. He paid in cash and returned to the car but hesitated as he unlocked it. He hadn't seen the Jeep following him. It had arrived from the opposite direction. He stowed his supplies on the passenger seat and got down onto his stomach, the hot tarmac almost burning through his T-shirt. The car smelled of fuel and oil and heat. He worked his way around the vehicle, pausing at the rear quarter with the bullet holes in the bodywork. He would have to admit that it was extremely noticeable, but he couldn't do much about it now. He got down on the ground again and studied the underside and found the device under the offside rear wheel arch. It was a plastic box with a magnetic strip glued to one side. A wire trailed out about three inches. He knew enough about explosives to know that there would not be enough plastic explosive to destroy the vehicle, and anybody worth his salt would have attached an explosive – especially this size – to the fuel tank. No, this was an entirely different matter. It was a tracker.

Lomu studied it, slowly formulating a plan. He decided to leave it in play and got back into the vehicle.

EIGHTEEN

Lomu parked in a space next to a stone wall, hiding the bullet holes from view and giving himself a good vantage point from which to view the entire carpark. From now on, he assumed he was under surveillance. He did not know his enemy – hopefully Neil Ramsay would help him with that – but surveillance and counter-surveillance was his bread and butter. If they wanted to play games with him, he would show them how to play. He had hunted ISIS and Al Qaeda, and he had deceived the Russian FSB, GRU and the SRV. He had tracked the Russian Bratva and other mafia families, and he had always come out on top.

He spotted his tail before he reached the marina. Black, Fijian, medium height and weight. He would guess the man to be in his late twenties. Lomu stood near a boat which had been hauled out of the water. The craft was a thirty-foot power boat with rakish writing and decals down the side and across the transom four 150 HP Suzuki outboards left little to the imagination regarding its purpose. Lomu photographed the boat, then posed for a selfie, but he had not reversed the lens and he photographed the man who was following him and the entire area around him as he changed poses and scanned the area. He continued towards the harbour master's office, checking the photographs as he went. When he enlarged the picture of the man, he could see the awkwardness in his eyes and the next few pictures showed the hesitation in his demeanour. He couldn't spot another suspect.

The harbour had become a marina in his twenty-year absence. Million-dollar yachts and speedboats glistened in a flotilla of white and stainless steel where wooden hulled fishing boats had once been moored, and beyond the channel in the lagoon, luxury cruise liners rose out of the water like floating tower blocks, a series of water taxis ferrying off a thousand tourists for a few hours sunburn on the beaches, and a tour of the local markets. Lomu no longer recognised the place. It had become a millionaires' playground and tourist mecca, and the harbour – the last bastion of working-class Fiji – like many beacons of tradition and heritage, had disappeared.

Lomu found what he wanted and studied the criteria. He did not hold any of the day skipper certification that was listed on the tariff board. But he did have large funds available, just as long as Ramsay had not put a block on his card. As he studied the tariff, further down the quay a tanned woman, lythe and athletic in build, with sun-bleached brown hair stepped out of a wooden hut holding a bunch of inflatable lifejackets in one hand a two-way radio in the other. She regarded him with scrutiny, then dropped the jackets on the ground and walked towards him, attaching the radio to the belt atop an incredibly short pair of white tailored shorts. The white showed up her bronzed skin, and Lomu realised he was staring at her a little too intently for anyone who had heard of *Me Too*.

"G'day big fella, how can I help 'ya?" she said lightly. Lomu knew that the twang to her accent could only mean she was Australian. "After a boat for this 'arvo?"

He nodded. "I've used plenty of boats, but I don't have the accreditation."

She smiled. "Well, you're like this fella I once knew who fell out of a twenty-storey window," she replied.

"So far, so good as he passed every floor?"

"No, just shit out of luck…"

"I only need a boat that will get me to Uluwala. I don't mind something small but paying for something twice the size," he ventured. "If that gets rid of the need for accreditation?"

"Like brush it aside?"

"Yeah."

"So, I make a load more money and turn a blind eye to your *paper* expertise?"

"That's right."

"And you'll pay a substantial deposit? You know, in case of an accident…"

"Absolutely."

She smiled. "Still shit out of luck, my friend."

He nodded. "I get the feeling I really *am* shit out of luck…"

"I thought I mentioned that?"

"Yeah, I got the gist of it."

"What's your name?"

He hesitated. "Davinder Lomu," he replied. "Dave to my friends."

"Well, *Dave*, you are in luck if you want to go to Uluwala. I'm just about to take a boat out there and pick up one for a service. I'll be on the island for around an hour or so. Maybe two. Suit you?"

"Yes," he replied, not even thinking it through for a second. Women didn't get much more attractive or personable in his opinion. Even if she had seen right through him and told him he was *shit out of luck* twice in as many minutes.

"Cool. Wait right here. I'll be back in ten."

Lomu nodded and watched her walk away. He didn't even know her name, but he certainly liked what he saw as she crossed the carpark, her long, tanned legs firm and unyielding. He shook his head. What the hell was he doing? He needed to concentrate. He was searching for his missing half-sister, and he not only had people taking pot shots at him, but he had a tail on him right now and a tracking device secreted on his vehicle. Now wasn't the time to admire an ass and a pair of legs.

He walked further down the quay and looked down at the water, which was clear and deep. He noted that it was far less oily than when the marina had been a fishing harbour. Shoals of tiny fish flicked in and out from the shadows of the boats and larger trigger fish swam close to the shoals waiting to snap. It couldn't be nice to be a tiny fish.

The woman came back with her sun-bleached hair bunched up under a white baseball cap, carrying a clip-board and a cooler. She smiled at Lomu and said, "I'm Jenny, by the way..."

"Nice to meet you. And thanks for this, I can chip in for fuel if you want."

She shook her head, scrunching her nose, which high-lighted a smattering of freckles. "No, the customer wants his boat back and another wants theirs taken away. No drama. Just hold on tight and enjoy the ride."

Lomu smirked, his lurid mind not sure if she had said

the last sentence with a sense of innuendo. Doubtful, he would admit, but he always lived in hope. He followed her down the quay to a wooden gangplank which was rather steep because of the low tide. He noted that even at low tide the marina had a substantial depth. He couldn't remember how deep the harbour had been as a child, but he suspected that the marina had been developed to accommodate the multi-million-dollar yachts with their keels and deep draught.

Jenny led them to a boat called *Ja Janna*. It was what was termed a fast fisher. A modern speedboat with a substantial cabin and clear deck space designed for fun, a fast pace but with a degree of practicality. Lomu noticed the twin 100 HP horsepower Evinrude outboards and knew that she would get him to Uluwala in good time. Jenny hopped up agilely and secured the cooler. "There's water and Minute Maid in there, if you want something to drink."

"Thanks," he replied. "Please let me give you something..."

"Don't worry, mate," she said lightly. "And if you know so much about boats, then you can cast off the bow once the engines are running..."

Lomu nodded and worked his way around the wheelhouse to the prow. He caught hold of the rope and unwound it from the cleat affixed to the pontoon keeping just enough pressure on the rope looped once around the cleat to keep the vessel steady. The twin Evinrude engines fired into life and Lomu waited for Jenny to give him the nod. She had put on a pair of Ray-Bans and nodded when she caught hold of the throttles. Lomu unhooked the rope and coiled it around his elbow before dropping it on the deck and working his way back around the wheelhouse. Jenny backed away from the pontoon, then swung the prow clear and engaged forward drive and the craft eased forward and out into what was clearly a channel, with boats on swinging moorings on either side facing the same way as the tide now made its way in. Jenny kept to a speed of around 5 knots until she cleared the boats and crossed between two buoys – one green and one red – and she immediately eased the throttles forward and the prow rose out of the water. Their speed gained rapidly, and the boat started to level up. Lomu noticed her using a small lever on the side of the control panel, and he knew this was the trim and tilt control, which changed the angle of the propellors and allowed the front of the boat to lower into the water and plane smoothly. They were soon travelling at two thirds throttle, around 28 knots. The ocean was calm and glassy and behind them, their wake cut a huge swathe in the surface, a three-foot wave peeling cleanly on either side.

Lomu welcomed the cool wind on his face, a pleasing relief from the oppressive heat back at the marina. The air felt easier to breathe, away from the petrol and diesel fumes and the smell of hot fibreglass, bait and seaweed.

"So, why the interest in Uluwala?" Jenny asked, her voice raised to compensate for both engine and wind noise.

Lomu shrugged. "Just interested, that's all."

She laughed. "This is a small place," she said. "Shabnam told me to look out for you." She paused. "She said you were going to try and get out to the island and that she would bet you'd start here at the marina."

He shook his head. Jenny's friendliness and kind gesture wasn't quite what it seemed. Or perhaps it was. Nothing here could be taken on face value. "Shabnam..." He paused. "Do you know her well?"

She nodded. "Her husband and my ex played tennis together. We got chatting one day at the club and struck up a friendship. She's a nice woman. Doesn't deserve to be caught up in all this."

"So, what do you know about *this*?"

Jenny shrugged. "Fiji is a great place. But it's an island. Or rather, hundreds of islands. Islands are like villages. You cross someone and everybody knows. You fuck someone you shouldn't, and news gets around fast. You have money problems, and the next thing you're a charity case. Small arena, small minds." She paused. "Take my ex, for example. He had an affair with a married woman, and he eventually had to leave. He was a real estate agent. The woman he had the affair with was the wife of a local solicitor. Pretty soon, he couldn't get conveyancing done, couldn't get the right permits, had less and less people use him..." She shrugged. "It killed his business because he was becoming ostracised. The bastard..." Lomu nodded, but how a man could have cheated on Jenny was beyond him. But then he remembered the great golfer Seve Ballesteros who while seated at a bar reputedly ignored the men around him as they all turned to watch a beautiful woman enter the bar and said, *"Somebody somewhere is already bored of her..."* A good reminder that beauty was only skin deep and that you never could tell what was going on with someone. "Shabnam deserves better from her superiors. Someone is taking McGregor's money to turn a blind eye. Well, not turn a blind eye, as such, more like cover up a murder and do nothing about a missing girl. It's outrageous!"

He nodded. He wondered exactly what the detective had said about him. Did she tell her that she was using a man whose half-sister had disappeared? Lomu was under no illusion that he was being used, it was just that because Shabnam had told other people about what he was doing here that he felt he had been hung out to dry. If he were to investigate McGregor and his organisation successfully, then he needed anonymity. Not become common knowledge to all and sundry. But he found himself shrugging it off just as quickly – he had now had way too many run ins with McGregor's machine to worry about tiptoeing along.

"What do you know about McGregor?" he shouted above the engine noise. "Anyway, I would think a development that will bring in thousands of tourists would only be a good thing for a boat charter company."

"These all-inclusive resorts do little for people like me," she replied quickly. "People stay in the resort and eat and drink their money's worth. They step outside for the odd excursion, but very few will hire a car and tour the island or make their way to someone like me. Only the more adventurous couples and families." She adjusted their course for a dingy tacking into the wind ahead of them, carving out a satisfying swathe in their wake as she maintained speed to avoid the tiny craft. "McGregor seems to have people in his pocket. There's no way a development like that should go ahead, especially as Kintoto Point is widely regarded as sacred and historical land. It is where the first Polynesian settlers were thought to have landed and started to farm." Lomu smiled. "Oh, yeah of course, I guess you already knew that," she said, unable to hide her embarrassment. "I do a potted history of the islands when I take out charters." She slowed the boat so rapidly that the three-foot wake washed into the transom and splashed them. The water was refreshingly cool and Lomu realised that his skin had been burning in the sun and the wind created by their speed. "Look!" she pointed.

Lomu stared to where she was pointing to portside. He shielded his eyes from the sun's glare, then noticed the tiny sprays of water. Dolphins. A pod of around two-dozen were arcing out of the water, their dorsal fins looking like a conveyer of cogs as another fin repeatedly took the other's place. Each time they breached the surface a puff of air along with a spray of water preceded the dorsal fin. It was quite hypnotic to watch, quite beautiful to behold. Jenny eased the throttle forwards and slowly headed around them on a course that would see them meet head on.

"What are you doing?" he asked, still watching the dolphins.

"Fancy a swim?" she asked, already tossing her baseball cap and sunglasses onto the seat and pulling off her shirt. Lomu stared at her breasts, barely contained by a string bikini top. She smiled. "Get your kit off, Dave. You're getting a free dolphin excursion. Punters can expect to pay hundreds for this..."

Lomu watched as the dolphins headed towards them. He had seen dolphins around the island many times, but he had never swum with a pod. The thought of this omission struck him as strange somehow, but then he realised that he had left home at sixteen. His time here had merely been in the blink of an eye. He wondered whether Marie had ever swum with dolphins, whether Josefa had taken her after he had stepped in and replaced their father.

"Jesus, you're miles away!" she chided, already wearing just a bikini and demonstrating that she often sunbathed practically naked. She rolled a rope ladder over the side and dived into the water.

Lomu stripped off his T-shirt and dropped his cargoes and kicked off his shoes. He wore only a pair of tight boxers, but there was nobody around for at least a mile and Jenny didn't seem the type to worry about inhibitions. He leapt rather than dived – he did want to retain the boxers after all – and stroked a few times underwater, appreciating the cool water against his skin, then surfaced near Jenny, who was treading water just in front of the lead dolphin.

"Go under when I do," she said. "Just take a breath and drop downwards, then try to hold yourself there. They should come over and check us out..."

Lomu nodded, happy to follow Jenny's lead. There was something so vibrant, sexy, fun and adventurous about her that he would probably have followed her anywhere. Her enthusiasm seemed contagious. He watched when she took a breath and lowered calmly out of sight. He took a deep breath and dipped under the surface, sculling with his hands by his sides to descend deeper. Jenny rested peace-fully in front of him, and he watched as the first dolphin swam effortlessly to her, gliding around her and then cruising towards him. Other dolphins did the same, and they were soon encircled by the creatures. Lomu needed more air, but Jenny seemed comfortable and continued to interact with them. He snatched a breath at the surface and dived back down, eager to pick up where he had left off, but the dolphins were already twenty metres away from where he had been, and he surfaced and swam front crawl towards the arcing fins and puffs of air and water.

Jenny swam to him, and they treaded water until she caught hold of his hand and said, "They're right below us, come on..." She held her breath and they descended together, hand in hand as the smaller members of the pod encircled them. Lomu reached out and stroked one, the skin soft and rubbery and warm. Jenny did the same, almost savouring the encounter. They surfaced and she kissed him on the lips, but before he could respond, she had dived back down, and he was left perplexed treading water on the surface. He dived under and swam to her, rather than the dolphins. She looked like a mermaid, her legs closed firmly, and just her lower legs working in unison to keep her steady, with the dolphins gliding gracefully around her. And then, in a flash, they were gone. She patted him on the shoulder and when they surfaced and gasped for air, she spluttered, "Let's get back to the boat. I don't like the way that they bugged out."

"Wait, what was the kiss about...?" he asked, but she was already stroking hard towards the boat. Lomu didn't need telling twice. He had seen giant tiger sharks growing up, and they were the main ones to fear, along with bulls and greater hammerheads. He dug in and soon caught up with Jenny, his arms and shoulders built for powering through the water. He could have overtaken her, but he felt that despite what had spooked the dolphins, racing past her to the boat would certainly negate a second kiss.

Jenny caught hold of the rope ladder and climbed agilely out. Lomu ducked his head under and checked three-sixty and downwards for sharks, then followed her out. As they stood dripping on the deck, there was no sign of anything in the water and the dolphins could be seen arcing two or three hundred metres in the distance.

"Sorry about that," she said. "I kind of got caught up in the moment. It was so beautiful, so spiritual, even." She paused. "Promise not to report me for sexual harassment?"

Lomu was about to laugh, but she looked serious. He smiled and said, "Just so you know, it would be alright anytime..."

She smiled. Looking at all six-feet-four and eighteen stone of him, muscular and dripping wet in nothing but his clinging boxers. She didn't even try and avert her gaze from the obvious. "We may need dinner first," she chided, picking up a small towel and wiping herself down. She tossed him the towel and pulled on her shorts, the fabric sticking on her damp skin and forcing her to do a little jiggle with her legs to get them on properly. She watched as he dried himself as best he could in a towel so small that it practically amounted to a flannel and pulled his cargoes over his wet boxer shorts. "I know a great seafood place, if you have time while you're out here?"

He couldn't really think about a date, but he guessed he had to eat. "Sound's great," he replied. "I'll take your number, if you don't mind, and give you a call." The moment of the kiss had gone, and Jenny already had her shirt on and was whipping the water out of her hair before hiding it under her baseball cap. He pulled on his T-shirt, his clothes already damp, but he would soon dry in the sun and the wind the boat would soon make them feel.

"I'll look forward to it," she replied, already reaching for the ignition and throttles. The engines fired into life and as she got on the throttles she said, "I think I know where you should start on Uluwula."

"Really?"

"Yes," she said, the boat building speed until they were soon at two thirds throttle and planing smoothly on the glassy surface. "The church," she said emphatically. "They're a religious bunch out here, and they have a display of old Fijian artifacts with the narrative much towards *simple natives*, rather than their country's heritage." She paused. "Many of the people on Uluwula are direct descendants from the original English and Dutch traders. They have resisted multicultural integration, for the most part at least."

Lomu nodded. He hadn't been to church in years. It was as good a place to start as any.

NINETEEN

It was hot now. Over thirty-five degrees and the sun was directly above him in a cloud-free sky. As he turned and looked back at the dock where Jenny was greeting the owner of the fast fisher, he noticed that the horizon was the same colour as the sky, and it appeared that either the sea or the sky went on forever, depending on which caught your eye first.

Lomu trudged the steps into the town. The houses were colonial style with influences of Portuguese, Dutch and British. The streets were narrow and cobbled, and thankfully funnelled a refreshing breeze a few degrees cooler than the openness of the harbour. Tourists sipped iced beverages at wobbly tables, studying maps and leaflets or perusing their phones. Lomu walked past, following Jenny's directions to the church, which he soon saw on top of a manmade hill in the centre of the town. The hill had been created from volcanic rock, coral and sand more than three-hundred years ago and vines, grass and soil derived from wind-borne dust and rotting vegetation had bound it all together. The edges of the hill were now well-manicured lawn and painstakingly tended terraces of plants that were all largely in flower, with blooms of purples, reds, yellows and blues. The church itself seemed out of character sat atop the hill in the middle of tropical paradise, and he supposed the town had been stubbornly constructed in specific styles depending on which settlers occupied at the time. Lomu climbed the steps out of the town and up to the church. He stopped on a bend in the path between flights of steps and looked back on the harbour and the main island beyond. The view was stunning, the millpond calm ocean reflecting the sun and azure cloudless sky. In the bay, he could see the pod of dolphins. They were no longer travelling but were swimming in circles feeding on a shoal of fish. The dolphins swum in formation, a large U-shape with the dolphins at the side swimming to-and-fro to steer the shoal, much as a whipper-in would have controlled a pack of hounds. All the while, dolphins zipped past the mouth of the U and snatched fish at the head of the shoal, then swapped position at the rear and flanks. A few tourists had paused behind him on the steps taking photographs and pointing at the sight. On the lower steps in front of them, two men stood awkwardly, not looking at the wonderous sight in the bay, yet with no interest in the church. Lomu stared directly at one of the men and smiled when the man looked away, scratched his head and decided to watch the bay. The other man stretched somewhat unbelievably – unnatural and over-compensating - and followed suit. Lomu sprinted the last few steps and turned the corner. He waited a count of three, then headed back. Both men stopped in their tracks mid-sprint half-way up the steps, and the game was up. Lomu remained where he was, humoured by the indecision on the men's faces and watched as they hurriedly took a path along one of the terraces and disappeared behind a large bush heavily blooming in resplendent red flowers. Lomu remembered one of the men from the marina carpark. He must have followed them in a boat of his own. And now the guy had back-up. Lomu couldn't recall seeing a boat following them, and nor did he notice other vessels in the vicinity when he and Jenny had swum with the dolphins. But he supposed that it wouldn't have taken a genius to deduce where they had been heading to, first by watching their course, and secondly because Mustafa and Monique had travelled to the island in their search to prove that the village lay on sacred ground.

It was clear that the men had been tasked to watch. If they wanted to kill him, then they could have been more proactive. Unless they were biding their time; waiting for an opportunity when there were no tourists about, no witnesses. Lomu could not see from the men's clothing whether they were armed. It was so easy to conceal a weapon - a folding knife in a pocket, or a small handgun in a kidney holster or even an ankle holster. He carried a folding multitool in his own pocket, and it was equipped with a wickedly sharp three-inch blade that locked firmly in place when opened. He had honed the blade with a whetstone and leather strop, and it was sharp enough to shave with, and he felt its comforting presence as he stepped into the cool shadows of the church and checked to see if his pursuers were paying attention.

Lomu wasn't a religious man, but he did appreciate the sense of calm and serenity he always experienced when he entered a church. There were times, like funerals and weddings and christenings when the atmosphere was commensurate with the occasion, but away from those events the calmness of a church was difficult to replicate elsewhere. The church was blessedly cool inside the stone walls with its high vaulted ceiling and his footsteps echoed as he walked across the stone floor, and as he looked around him the entire cavernous structure was deserted. He suspected the tourists were still watching the sight of the dolphins in the bay, but soon they would make their way into the church. He couldn't decide whether that would be a good thing, or bad. His pursuers would want to avoid doing anything in public. But he could do with some privacy as he looked around.

There was nothing at the alter that looked remotely helpful to his cause, and nor at the parapet. The pews were basic, austere. Quaker style furniture that was entirely perfunctory and both upright and squared at the edges. Not even a simple cushion for kneeling in prayer. The windows were created from stained glass depicting scenes from the New Testament and several of the panes had been broken and replaced with clear glass. Lomu suspected that stained glass was a lost skill, and not readily available throughout Oceania. He checked the tapestries and icons hanging from the walls, and soon found himself at the rear of the church as the first of the tourists wandered inside. Cameras and smartphones clicked away, and the few people who had entered milled around not sure what they were looking at and no doubt thought the dolphin watching was time better spent.

At the rear of the church a series of tables behind a velvet rope contained artifacts including pottery, figurines carved from bone and whale tooth, and jewellery made from pearls, shells and shark's teeth. There were framed information guides describing what each artifact was, along with early photographs of Fijian tribes' people taken at the turn of the nineteenth century. Lomu studied the artifacts, then looked up as the group of tourists filtered out of the open doorway, apparently uninterested in the rest of what seemed to be a church identical to a thousand others throughout Europe. Lomu noted a framed document which read:

When Fiji's first settlers arrived from the islands of Melanesi at least 3,500 years ago, they carried with them a wide range of food plants, the pig, and a style of pottery known as Lapita ware. That pottery is generally associated with peoples who had well-developed skills in navigation and canoe building and were horticulturists. From Fiji the Lapita was carried to Tonga and Samoa, where the first distinctively Polynesian culture evolved. Archaeological evidence suggests that two other pottery styles were subsequently introduced into Fiji, though it is not clear whether they represent major migrations or simply cultural innovations brought by small groups of migrants. In most areas of Fiji, the settlers lived in small communities near ridge forts and practiced a slash-and-burn type of agriculture. In the fertile delta regions of southeast Viti Levu however, there were large concentrations of population. Those settlements, which were based on intensive taro cultivation using complex irrigation systems, were protected by massive ring-ditch fortifications.

The European discoveries of the Fijian island group were accidental. The first of these discoveries was made in 1643 by the Dutch explorer, Abel Janzsoon Tasman, who sighted the north-east fringe. In 1774 Captain James Cook passed the south-eastern islands and made further explorations in the eighteenth century. Captain William Bligh travelled through the island group in his open longboat after the mutiny on HMS Bounty in 1789 and later returned to explore further in 1792.

When Christian missionaries landed in the Fijian

islands in the late eighteenth century they were promptly killed and eaten by the locals. Despite their ability to grow and farm food, Cannibalism has a long history in the Fijian islands, which were previously known as the Cannibal Islands. According to the Fiji Museum, there is archaeological evidence to suggest that the practice of consuming human flesh dates back more than 2,500 years here. In artifacts 9 through to 13, you will see ancient flint and obsidian knives. These knives are more than ten times sharper than a modern surgical scalpel, and human bones have been excavated on various archaeological digs with deep lacerations indicative of butchery to cleave muscle from bone, rather than injury sustained in tribal warfare. By 1854, having stamped out the practice of cannibalism, Methodist missionaries had also brought most Fijians under the influence of the Christian faith. Roman Catholic and Anglican missionaries arrived later but did not enjoy the same success. By the 1860s Fiji was attracting European settlers, intent on establishing plantations to capitalize on a boom in cotton prices caused by the American Civil War. Disputes ensued over land and political power within and between European and Fijian communities, and problems arose with labourers introduced from other Pacific islands. Those factors contributed to violent confrontations, exacerbated the implicit instability of Fijian society, and ensured that no Fijian chief could impose his rule on the whole group. European attempts at government were doomed by the greed and factionalism of their members and by the interference of European governments and consuls. Imperial intervention thus became inevitable.

Artifact no. 22 is a silver coin in the shape of a half-moon believed to indicate the lunar influence of planting crops, and on the tide to maximise fishing success. It is not known whether coins like these were in common circulation, or whether it was intended to be used as a piece of jewellery. The coin was carbon dated to circa 500BC and looks to have been crudely shaped, with nicks taken out of its flat edge. On the reverse side (see photo) the depiction is of a partial mountain, a partial sun and the inscription translates as: **Degei** *(pronounced Ndengei)* **mountain the light forever**. *It is speculated to be one half of a coin, but archaeologists still debate this as there have been no other coins found of the same era, and it would be more probable that the coin was in fact a medallion or talisman. There is no record of a mountain being named after Degei, either.*

Lomu's blood ran cold. He felt the shiver run up his spine and somewhat bizarrely, the nape of his neck flushed hot, as if every possible sensory reflex wanted him to take notice, but he already had. He had seen something like this curious looking coin hanging on the wall for all to see in McGregor's study. Amid the egotistical bullshit of McGregor's curios that were Hemingway's fountain pens, typewriter and gun, the macabre sight of the heads or 'trophies' of slaughtered animals on the wall and the collection of Aboriginal boomerangs and war clubs, a single sliver of metal affixed to a length of leather cordage had caught his eye. He looked tentatively around him, another tourist was just leaving for something more interesting, something more *Fijian* than an Anglican church on a manmade hill of coral. The talisman was behind a piece of glass, and he could not see any wires, but that did not mean that it wasn't alarmed. But where was the warden, the vicar or the security? He stepped inside the rope and immediately wished he hadn't. An alarm sounded and without hesitation, he picked up a solid piece of wood that looked like a miniature caveman's club. The key had said that it was a 'last rites' used by fishermen, and Lomu had seen and used plenty in his youth. A sturdy little club for stunning line-caught fish before taking them off the hook. He hammered it into the toughened glass, surprised it merely cracked, then went to town on the glass. Eighteen stone of muscle and it took a dozen attempts before the toughened glass shattered. Lomu snatched the coin and pocketed it as he ran across the slate floor and out into the bright Fijian sun, and directly into the two men.

One of them pulled a switchblade and the six-inch blade flashed out, glinting in the sun. Lomu, the 'last rites' still in his hand, swung savagely and the knife spun through the air, flung from the man's shattered hand to the tune of him screaming an agonising wail. He clasped his hand and hopped from foot to foot as he wailed, the sight quite humorous, had it not been for the diving knife in the other man's hand. The second man, a full head shorter than Lomu and about half as wide, seemed to make the right assessment of the situation and caught hold of his companion and the two men sprinted and scrabbled on the loose gravel surface to the path leading through the terraced gardens. Lomu wasted no time, sprinting to the steps and through the group of tourists who had briefly paused their vigil towards the dolphins in the bay, looking for the source of the alarm.

Lomu was down the steps and into the warren of colonial houses lining the shady streets of the town in less than a minute. He slipped through one alleyway and then another, until he was back on the quayside and searching for Jenny among the scattering of tourists who had just disembarked from water taxis from the main island. He found her leaning on a dinghy and completing the paperwork for her collection. Her shapely, tanned legs and short-cut white captains' shorts were almost enough for him to take his eye off the ball, and he spun around and surveyed the harbour and groups of people mingling about quite aimlessly in that way all tourists do. He did not see either man and was quite surprised that he could no longer hear one of the men wailing from his shattered hand.

"Hi," Jenny said breezily when she looked up from the clipboard. "Find what you were looking for?"

"Perhaps," he replied. "How did you know to suggest where to look?"

She smiled. "I know things."

He walked up to her and said quite coldly, "Don't mess about with me. You suggested I start in the church. You know Shabnam, who has got me running around doing her work for her, what is all of this about?"

She straightened and stared back at him. He could tell that she was angered, even though the Ray-Ban wraparound sunglasses shielded her eyes. "I'm just trying to help a friend, and help you," she replied icily. "I don't like big development screwing over the little guy, either."

Lomu removed the piece of metal from his pocket, holding it in his open palm, the sun glinting off it. "There is another piece like this in McGregor's study. How did you know?"

"Christ, you stole it..."

"Borrowed..."

Jenny turned and walked to the edge of the quay. It was constructed from square-cut stone and looked to Lomu like the harbour at Charlestown in Cornwall, one of the filming locations for the TV series *Poldark*. It looked quite out of place in tropical Fiji, but no different to the colonial Caribbean he supposed. People tended to build what they knew, not what was practical. An eighteenth-century tall ship would not have looked out of place moored within the stone walled harbour, had it not already been brim-full of modern white pleasure craft. "I'll tell you when we're underway. Judging from that alarm and the people gathering on the edge of the town, the police will be here any moment..." She dropped down the ladder into a fast-looking craft called *Diva* powered by an inboard engine and complete with swim deck over the twin propellers. Lomu followed suit. As before, he made his way to the prow and got ready to cast off. "Dan Carter is my uncle," she replied, looking at the expression of surprise on Lomu's face. She started the engine and it purred into life, with just a hint of rawness as she edged forward the throttle and whipped her line over the stanchion. "Trust me, it's coincidence that he's here," she said, raising her voice above the building engine revs. Lomu gathered the loose rope and dropped it onto the deck and made his way back to her. "I left Oz and worked in Tahiti for a while, then Tonga. I like the Pacific Islands, the feel to them. I've travelled quite a bit, and Oceania is like a chilled Caribbean. Not that they aren't chilled there, but there's always a sense of tension and poverty and a mix of people who embrace tourism, and an undercurrent of revolt and hatred for the years of slavery and colonialism." She shrugged. "Can't blame them, I suppose."

"And Shabnam knows that Dan Carter is your uncle?"

"Of course."

"Then why help her?" he asked. "Blood's blood, when all's said and done."

"Not when that *blood* touched you up as a teen..."

"Right..."

She sighed. "First off, he's my mother's cousin," she explained. "I always called him uncle growing up. When I got to fourteen, he made me feel uncomfortable with the way he always looked at me. When I was fifteen, his comments were downright inappropriate, and I couldn't go near him without him groping me. Catching an ass cheek, or even my breasts. At seventeen he cornered me at a family barbeque and..." She took a breath and said heavily, "He put his hand down my knickers and did all that entails..."

"I'm sorry," Lomo replied, as if his apology went for all the wrong doings of every man. He said nothing more, realising how dumb he had sounded, how empty his words could be construed.

"I avoided him like the fucking plague after that. I didn't come home from uni much, and at twenty-one I crewed yachts around the world for two years. I avoided my family just to avoid seeing him. He's a wrong-un for sure. He got chucked out of the army, couldn't hold down jobs, there were rumours he robbed a bank and that he worked as a mercenary in Africa, then he got involved with McGregor and he soon ended up with a lot of money and working on projects all around the world. He's McGregor's hatchet man. The guy who sorts out problems, so that McGregor can keep his hands clean and live like Croesus." She paused. "I avoided that bastard for ten years, then he rocks up here like nothing happened and wants to get reacquainted." She shook her head. "It was the way he said it, the way he looked. Like he'd had a sample of the goods, now wanted the whole thing..." She hammered the throttle forward and the bow rose until she worked the trim and tilt lever and they got onto a flat plane as they passed the speed marker buoys and entered the bay. "I still can't stand to be touched down there," she said shaking her head. "Not with fingers, at least..." She shrugged, realising she had probably said too much, but it was out there now. "I went to McGregor's mansion to confront Dan, tell him to stay the fuck away from me. Instead, I got the tour of his master's castle, and warned that he would be just as powerful one day, and that I should consider not making waves. That it would be a good set up for me, to take up with a rich, older man who legally wasn't blood relative enough to cause problems. Legal or breeding-wise. Christ, I almost vomited on the bastard's feet!" She paused. "But it wasn't until I taxied Mustafa and Monique to Uluwula that I realised the significance of the metal medallion I had seen on McGregor's study wall. They felt that they had gotten nowhere and told me about what they had seen in the church, showed me some photos taken on Monique's phone, I instantly recognised the piece..."

Lomu rolled his eyes. "And you told them where you had seen another just like it..."

"I did. I'm sorry, but I never realised what would happen..."

"Of course, you didn't," he replied, resting his giant palm on her shoulder.

"But I told Shabnam, and by then she said there was some kind of corruption in the case, and she couldn't go in all guns blazing..."

Lomu nodded. *But he could...*

Jenny adjusted the boat's throttle and steered around an imaginary obstruction.

"What are you doing?" he asked.

She glanced behind her and adjusted their course again. "There's a boat gaining on us. If I didn't move, their course would have them hit us," she replied and Lomu looked behind them. "But I've adjusted, and they're still coming right for us..."

TWENTY

They were making close to 40 knots, or 46 mph. On water, that was fast. Twice the speed needed for water skiing or wakeboarding. The boat was gaining on them as Jenny put down the last travel of throttle and the craft maxed out at 45 knots.

"They've got a fast RIB!" she shouted against the wind. The sound of the pursuing boat's engine pitch changed, and she glanced back at them, now only twenty metres from them, and bouncing crazily in their wake. If they gained much more distance, they would surely come crashing down upon them. "Hold on!" she shouted and Lomu grabbed the handle on the console next to him, stiffening his legs and bracing his feet for any sudden movement.

Jenny swung to port, and yanked back hard on the throttles, the RIB – or Rigid Hull Inflatable Boat – flew past them, and Jenny steered hard to starboard and powered the throttle forwards. The RIB turned quickly, too. Lomu grabbed the boat hook from its holder on the portside and took a swing at one of the men. He could tell that it was the man whose hand he had busted in the church, and he guessed it wasn't the man's day as the boat hook cracked against the man's skull. It wasn't a sharpened tool – designed entirely for hooking rope or pushing away from docks or other boats - but the head of the hook was made from plastic-coated metal with a rounded end to it, and it certainly did the job. The man fell forwards and collapsed in the hull of the RIB. The man at the helm hesitated for a moment, then clearly decided to continue with the pursuit, powered the throttles of the twin 250 HP outboards forwards and was soon perilously close to them as Jenny zig-zagged, skipping the speedboat across the water. Lomu had noticed that their boat was called a Four Winns 260. Near the rear of the boat on the blue and white paintwork just above the plimsol line it had simply read 250 HP in black lettering. He knew a little about fast boats from his time in the SAS as well as working with the SBS – the regiment's Royal Navy waterborne equivalent - but it did not take a genius, nor a professional skipper to realise they were seri-ously down on power compared to their pursuers.

"What's in the cuddy?" he shouted above the engine noise.

"A chemical toilet, life jackets, flares, rope and anchor..." she replied, carving out a new direction. Then she screamed when a gunshot drowned out the engine noise for a terrifying split second. She ducked instinctively, as did Lomu, who was now crouched and facing their attackers.

"No gun?" he asked somewhat hopefully.

"I'm afraid not..." Lomu watched as the man attempted to steady a shotgun and fire it one-handed. He nudged the wheel and the boat flipped to starboard as Jenny protested. "Careful! You'll tip us over!"

The gunshot rang out, the shot went wide and ahead of them the water looked like it was being rained upon over an area of three-square feet as the lead shot scattered. The man struggled to reload the weapon, his colleague now on his knees and rubbing his head with his one good hand.

"I thought the anchor was in the bow?"

"It is. It's always a good idea to have a spare. I know a guy and his buddy who went out without one and got well and truly in the shit when their engine got swamped by a freak wave and they ended up washed onto rocks. I insist on having two anchors on any boat I use."

Lomu did not reply. He was already staggering across the deck towards the cuddy doorway, the bare bones of a plan in his head. He grabbed the anchor and the coil of rope and set about untucking the end of the rope from the coil. He dropped it onto the deck, then almost tipped over the side when Jenny suddenly changed course. There was another gunshot, and the shot peppered the transom. Jenny screamed, then swore loudly and changed course and speed again. Lomu hung on tightly for all he was worth, but he pulled out the anchor and chain and tossed it onto the deck and unwound the length of rope from its recess. He used his multitool to slice through the rope a few feet from where it was fastened in the anchor compartment, then set about tying both ropes together.

"Ok, here's what I want you to do..." He paused. "Carve out a couple of S-turns, then straighten your course and increase speed to maximum..."

"I'm close to that now!" she shouted back at him. "And what about the gun?"

"Leave that to me..."

Lomu worked his way down to the stern, Jenny's S-turns more difficult to retain balance against than he had anticipated. He caught hold of the spare anchor because it looked to be the heaviest. The anchor from the anchor compartment was shiny and sharp-looking. It had a swivel crown and the two flukes set only on one side looked like the sharpened ends of a pickaxe. The contraption was designed to drop into the deep folded, then opened upon striking the seabed. The flukes would then dig into the seabed and the drifting boat would pull tension on the rope, swinging the anchor around and enabling the flukes to dig in. Lomu had already weighed up the most suitable anchor for his intentions and he turned and nodded at Jenny as she straightened the craft's direction and pushed forward on the throttle. "Hold her steady!" he yelled against the wind buffeting him in the face.

The RIB gained on them quickly. The man with the run of bad luck was now on his feet, favouring his right hand and holding on for dear life with the other. He could not operate the gun, and nor could the man on the helm, although he tried but seemed to struggle aiming it as the boat pounded up and down in their wake. Lomu threw the boat hook like a blunt spear, striking the driver and causing him to drop the weapon. The other man bent down to retrieve it, but Lomu had already thrown the first anchor over the transom close to the approaching RIB's prow before he straightened back up with the shotgun in his one good hand. The rope uncoiled at Lomu's feet in a blur. It was already close to the adjoining knot when he picked up the other anchor, the rope spooling out rapidly. With just thirty or forty feet of rope remaining, he tossed the anchor over the prow of the RIB and waited just a few short seconds for physics to do everything else. The first anchor had dug in hard on the coral seabed, and when the rope pulled tight, the second anchor ripped into the hull, caught fast, puncturing several air compartments, and the boat was stopped-dead from close to fifty-knots in a fraction of a second. The prow went under the water and the entire boat flipped over and disappeared under the surface. Lomu watched as the inflatable boat worked like a giant fishing float and resurfaced fifty feet further back from where it had gone under. It bobbed like a cork, its heavy engines above the water but no longer running, and when it finally settled, it did so upside down with no sign of either man at the surface.

"Do we stop?" Jenny asked, easing back on the throttle, her eyes on the sight behind them.

"No," he replied, watching a sizeable cruiser heading their way. The two men had made their intentions all too clear. Lomu was past the point of showing any quarter to his enemy. If the approaching vessel found the men alive, then they could take it from there. He looked at Jenny and said, "No, we do not stop."

TWENTY-ONE

Lomu stopped the car in a layby on the hill overlooking the bay with the island of Uluwula a distant haze on the horizon. Barely perceptible as a landmass, the island looked like a bank of mist or dark cloud more than twenty miles away.

He got out of the vehicle, got onto his stomach and pulled out the tracker. He studied it for a moment, then coiled the two trailing wires around it and tossed it over the edge of the cliff into the sea. He had plans later, and he did not want them knowing where he was. He was done playing games. He slipped back into the driver's seat and opened a bottle of water. He was hot and perspiring and needed a cold shower or another swim. He thought about swimming with the dolphins, but mostly he thought about Jenny and her string bikini.

Lomu looked at the phone on the seat beside him. The caller ID told him that it was Ramsay, although he had somewhat humorously, though unkindly entered his name as *Mr Bean*. As he answered, opened the door and stepped out noticing a breeze in the trees. "Neil, thanks for getting back to me..."

"You've got a few problems there," he replied getting straight to the point and not bothering with the customary greeting.

"Tell me about it," replied Lomu tersely.

"I am." There was a long pause and Lomu could hear Ramsay tapping away on a keyboard. Eventually, he said, *"McGregor, fifty-six years of age, first name Sebastian, has business interests all around the Pacific basin, including South Korea and Japan. Everything from cabbage farms and a company making jars of kimchi in South Korea to tuna processing plants in Japan. Not as dolphin friendly as most people would prefer, either. And by the way, that pickled cabbage... kimchi... is the new wonder food. His stocks are high."*

"He said that he had pineapple plantations in Australia," Lomu told him. "That he employed *blacks* to do the work..."

"Yes. And he also owns pineapple plantations in Hawaii. In all, he has one hundred and seventeen businesses. From opal mining in the Northern Territories, to coal mining in Indonesia. He skirts the law and has regular run-ins with local governments and the environmental lobby, but technically he seems legitimate."

"But if we dig deeper...?"

"I have no doubt he's a truly bad egg."

Lomu smiled at Ramsay's take on him. "And Carter?"

Ramsay paused. *"Be careful of that one, Dave. Dan Carter was in the Australian army and did a stint with the Australian SAS. He was thrown out for theft. Tens of thousands of dollars went missing, as did a clerk. The clerk was never found, and without the clerk there wasn't enough to pin the theft fully on Carter, but the general consensus was that he was as guilty as sin. Many believe he had something* to do with the clerk's disappearance, but again, not enough evidence. Incidentally, a couple of SAS soldiers took it upon themselves to pay Carter a visit and exact some caveman style justice, and neither man was seen again. Again, there wasn't enough to pin anything on him, and again, people close to the investigation all felt he was guilty."

"I don't doubt it," Lomu replied.

"He's also been banned entry from Thailand for alleged underaged sex. So-called sex tourism. He claims it was a misunderstanding, naturally."

Lomu seethed as he thought of his sexual assault on Jenny. "That sounds about right."

"Carter also did a spell in Africa. The usual tourist hotspots such as the Congo, Burkina Faso, Mali and Angola. Forget what the Russians are doing out there with the Wagner Group, this lot were out and out war criminals. Thousands slain for the diamond mining companies, oil companies and governments putting down the political opposition. In fact, his name comes up in countless Interpol investigations, but again..."

"Nothing that can be pinned on him successfully?"

"That's right." Ramsay paused. "But forget all that, it's his home country where he has done the most damage. Aboriginal Australians. Again, not directly, but it has been claimed that he has destroyed villages, even entire towns, by stealing water, creating drought, killing cattle and starting bushfires. The native Australians eventually move out and Carter claims the land, buys up the rights and sells it to... guess who?"

"McGregor..."

"Exactly. And we're not talking just a few settlements, either. The Australian government... any Australian govern-ment in the last six decades... have been catastrophically poor *in recognising racism and indigenous heritage. Worse than Britain and the Windrush affair, the land down under hasn't recognised Australian heritage and has segregated on the same level as apartheid in the very darkest days in South Africa history, except they were better at hiding it from the rest of the world. And they hid it in plain sight. They made it virtually impossible for native Australians to keep their traditions, forcing them to move to the cities for work and slowly turn their backs on their heritage."* Lomu knew the feeling. And it looked like McGregor and Carter were instigating the same agenda at Kintoto Point. Were the Fijian government secretly behind them? Backing the dilution of heritage in favour of putting people into the system? Shabnam had spoken of people inside the police and government being on McGregor's payroll. Maybe the development was backed at such a level that anything the families did would be in vain. He thought about the attempts on his life so far, the fact that whoever was behind this had no qualms about involving innocent people like the people mown down at the cookout and Jenny on the journey back from Uluwula, and of course the young Mustafa and the missing Monique. *"If you're up against this chap McGregor and his stooge, Dan Carter, then you'd better be prepared. Personally, Dave, I think you should get on a plane and come back to work."*

"I can't," He replied. "Not yet."

"Live to fight another day, my friend..." Lomu had never heard Neil Ramsay mention friendship before. He never usually gave advice, either. But he knew that the man had merely given him the salient facts. There was no doubt that Dan Carter was a hard nut to crack, and there was never any guarantee he would. The man certainly had the training and experience, and he definitely had the guile and

ruthlessness to go with it. Maybe he should heed the warning. Maybe he should give it all up as a lost cause. After all, he hadn't seen his family in twenty years and too much time had run. King had been right, albeit by proxy through Thomas Wolfe and his novel *You Can't Go Home Again.* Some things cannot be relived nor rekindled. *"What do you say, Dave? Coming back?"* Ramsay asked. *"I have plenty of work for you to get your teeth into."*

Lomu looked out across the bay. The sky was clear, azure blue and vast. The sea mirrored the sky and the sun cast a golden hue towards the beach. The sand as white as icing sugar. Below him, sugar cane fringed with palms spread down the mountainside like the baize on a snooker table. The wind on his face was cool enough to keep perspiration at bay. "What's the weather like in London?" he asked.

"Grey," Ramsay replied.

"How warm?" Lomu asked, knowing already what April was like in the city.

"Sixteen degrees. Cloudy. It's been drizzling. Why?"

Lomu smiled. He had no intention of getting on a plane just yet.

TWENTY-TWO

Lomu stopped the car as he neared the point. A few of the villagers were heading out in dug-out canoes, men paddling while their boys readied the nets. He recalled doing the same thing as a child with both his father and Josefa. When he was older and inevitably larger, he would paddle the canoe. The nets never needed readying – they were emptied, untangled and mended each time they were hauled in – and he had soon realised that the task was merely to give him and the other boys familiarity and ownership over the trip. A responsibility that they would take seriously. He felt a pang of emotion and nostalgia as he watched the canoes heading out to meet the end of the pushing tide out over the reef.

He started the car and entered the village, parking outside Marie's house. He wondered whether she would ever come clean about her husband's absence, but she was a proud woman and he guessed that he did not have the kind of relationship with her where she felt she could share. He supposed that would come, but only if he stuck around. He saw Marie heading to her car with a carrier bag. She looked at him, waved and put the bag in her car.

"Another food-run?" he asked.

She nodded. "I do what I can."

He nodded, knowing that without her husband things must be tight. "Can I help at all?"

"No need," she replied. "I just give a few leftovers, that's all."

"I mean, financially. Shabnam told me about your husband. It must be tough..."

"She had no right to tell you!" she snapped. "And don't play the big brother now; you're about twenty years too late!"

Lomu shrugged. "I guess I just wanted to know the reasoning for wanting me out here."

"Well, it wasn't for your bank account," she said acidly. "I just thought, with Josefa dying and all, you might like to make peace. Oh, and help find your half-sister who you've never seen, nor seem to care about..."

Lomu held up his hand. "Okay! I get it, I'm a shit brother..." He paused, noting the anger in her eyes. "I'm just trying to help." And then he looked at her earnestly. "He's really dying? I thought..."

She shrugged. "It's not going well, Davinder. What else can I say?" She looked up as a vehicle pulled over the grass and parked. Her face fell, and she got into her own vehicle and said, "We're running out of time. Monique is in danger, and we need to act now. McGregor needs taking down, and we'll do it. With or without you." She started the engine and pulled away, the tyres spinning on the sand and patches of grass.

"I'm beginning to think she doesn't like me..." Shabnam

said as she walked closer. "I hear you had an interesting visit to Uluwula."

Lomu smiled. "You've spoken to Jenny already?"

"Just passing."

"So, what do you know?" he asked. He was never in the habit of volunteering anything to the police. He had found he kept his freedom better that way.

"Not a great deal," she replied. "I think she is more than a little smitten with you, so she became somewhat evasive." She studied his expression but received nothing in return. "You found what you wanted at the church and ran into some trouble on the way back."

"You could say that."

"Both men were rescued by a passing pleasure craft. They were lucky, bruised, shaken and half-drowned by the time the boat picked them up. Unfortunately, they disappeared as soon as they made port. So, we don't know who they were, or what they wanted with you."

"But you know who they work for..."

"Conjecture," she replied. "That's what a judge would say." She paused. "Incidentally, what can you remember about the two men who jumped you? Other than you thought that they were fishermen."

Lomu shrugged. "One was black, five-feet ten, medium build. The other was of Indian descent, five-eight, heavier set. Both were Fijian. They drove a Mitsubishi pickup truck. White. Full of fishing kit – buoys, canes with flags, lobster pots and nets in the rear. Why?"

"They're dead. Both men were run off the road up in the mountains."

"Fishermen rarely go into the mountains," Lomu replied. "They don't tend to get a lot of fishing done that far from the sea..."

"Exactly."

"Accident?"

"I don't think so, but difficult to prove. Their vehicle was all burned up."

"Then it's my fault," he said sombrely. "One of them told me that they'd been put up to it." He paused, shaking his head despondently. "The man I questioned was fearful that they should not know that he talked. And now it's obvious why."

"It would appear so." Shabnam looked up as a small SUV drove up. "Your cousin's here," she announced. "I don't think she likes me very much, either."

Lomu watched as Delilah parked the little Suzuki and watched them both hesitantly. He waved at her, and she seemed to relax. She got out, carrying some groceries and walked them into Marie's bure. When she came back outside, she shrugged and walked over to them.

"I was hoping to catch Marie..."

"She's gone on a food-run. One out, one in. You're certainly looking after your own," he replied.

"I just got Marie the essentials. I'm trying to help while Jake is... away," she said, looking hesitantly at Shabnam. "We do what we can to help each other. It's our way of life."

Shabnam smirked. "Well, if that was for my benefit, it certainly stung." She paused. "Tell me, how is life in the city living in your apartment with the fulltime job in tourism? Biting the hand that feeds, aren't you?"

"Ouch..."

"Now, ladies..." Lomu grinned. "Come on, play nicely..."

"I was leaving, anyway," said Shabnam. She looked at Lomu and said, "But before I go, I'd like a private word." Delilah scoffed, spun around and stormed back to Marie's bure. Shabnam smiled at her reaction in much the same way a parent would an errant teen set upon making waves and protesting injustice at every opportunity. "Are you going to McGregor's mansion again?"

Lomu nodded. "There's something I need to check on."

"Yes, I thought there might be..." she nodded. "Good luck, and remember, I'm on the end of a phone if you run into any problems."

Lomu nodded and watched her go. He had come back to see if he could mend things with Marie, and she had left in a hurry again.

You can't go home again...

He looked around him. The village was empty. A few chickens pecked and scratched at the dirt and there was a pig tied to a spike in the ground, exploiting the shade of a palm at the end of its twenty feet of rope. It looked hot and fed up and if the feast had been anything to go by, was probably missing its companion. But that was how he had grown up. He had collected eggs and fished with his father and Josefa, while his mother wrung the occasional chicken's neck after it could no longer lay good eggs, but she would make the sacrifice last for most of the week, sometimes boiling the bones a second time to make a good soup or stock. Nothing was wasted, not even the vegetable peelings, which fed the chickens and when their manure was spread on the various veg patches around the village, it completed the circle. His family had not known vacuum packed meat, or frozen vegetables. Fish was in abundance and the only things they purchased had been spices and coffee and tea, as well as Lomu's beloved Milo.

Lomu looked out at the ocean, watching the tiny boats and canoes on the reef, and suddenly remembered his grandfather taking him out in his dugout canoe to catch a shark. The old man had used a length of bamboo split down the middle and the length of his forearm. In the centre of the bamboo a hole allowed a rope to go through, which was configured in a loop. The loop was played out and his grandfather inserted his arm in the channel of the bamboo as a guard. He then put his arm in the water and patted the surface of the water with his canoe paddle. Eventually an inquisitive and sizeable white tip reef shark, sensing a creature in distress, came to look for an easy meal, but instead found itself lassoed. His grandfather pulled the noose tight, the bamboo acting as a guard for his arm against gnashing teeth, then heaved the shark into the boat, where he bludgeoned it to death with his own 'last rites' club. Lomu remembered being in awe of the man as he hauled in a shark almost as big as the canoe. The practice was as old as the people of Oceania, but by the time Lomu had left the islands, his father's generation no longer hunted sharks in such a manner, and he imagined that nowadays sharks were barely hunted at all. Such was the impact of Chinese, Russian and Japanese factory fishing vessels that claimed millions of sharks each year, often discarding all but the fins back to the deep. A barbaric act that was kept alive solely by the Chinese and their taste for shark fin soup, and traditional Chinese medicine.

Lomo trudged along the familiar path, with the ocean on his right. Being one of the older houses, his family home was situated around a hundred metres further up the beach from Marie's. He could already see that it had been greatly modernised, with a new deck and a slate roof. The bure was raised on stilts and underneath had become a dumping ground for fishing equipment and a broken canoe. Outside was a pickup truck that had been new when Lomu left the island. He was surprised it was still running, and the only way he could tell it was the same truck was because it had the same jagged scratch running its entire length from bumper to bumper. Not his finest moment. Teenage angst and vitriol at its worst. As he walked past the truck, he felt a pang of guilt and shame. And regret.

He found his mother on the porch seated in her favourite rocking chair staring out at the infinity of the ocean horizon. There was a wistful look in her eye, and he wondered what she was remembering. She seemed so much older and had aged far more than he ever imagined she would have in twenty years. The saddest thing of all was he would never get those years back. She looked up at him, frowned like she didn't remember him, then eventually smiled warmly.

"Davinder," she said, beckoning him over to her. "Come, sit with me..."

Lomu strode over and took the five wooden steps up to the veranda in two easy strides. He pulled out a rickety-looking cane chair and sat it a few feet from his mother's side. "Where's Josefa?" he asked.

His mother sighed. "He has gone into the city and is dropping leaflets with Monique's photograph on them. Delilah had them printed at her work." She paused. "I can't seem to do anything... my will... it's all but gone." Tears filled her eyes and rolled steadily down her cheeks, but she did not sob. Lomu held his mother's hand, and she squeezed his own tightly. "It is Mustafa's funeral service in two days," she said quietly. "I'm not sure I can face it. Not with Monique still missing, and knowing what happened to that poor little pup..."

Lomu nodded, a smile of fondness cracking his tight lips. His mother had always called the children in the village 'pups', but not after the offspring of dogs, but of the shoals of shark pups that swam in shallow waters for safety from the predators on the reef. "Marie didn't say."

His mother shook her head. "Marie has too much going on. Monique disappearing, her husband..." she trailed off.

"I know that he's in prison."

"Oh." She paused. "That surprises me. Marie is proud. Too proud to go around mentioning things like that."

"Somebody else told me."

"I see." She looked at him and said, "Mustafa's parents told us that the upcoming funeral and all expenses had been paid by someone anonymously."

"That's nice."

"Would you know anything about that?"

"No," he lied.

She did not reply, instead turned her gaze once more to the sea. "I see him out there sometimes," she said. "Your father. I know I'm just imagining it, but it seems real enough to me. He's paddling the canoe and you're fiddling with the net. You used to get it in such a tangle with the nets, but he never minded. He was just pleased to be spending time with you."

"I know I left on bad terms," he said quietly. "I was just hurt. And then I was stubborn, I suppose."

"That's putting it lightly, Davy." She sobbed. "Twenty years..."

"It wasn't just like that. I had a career. I fought in two wars. Five tours, and God knows how many operations." He paused. "The time just started to pass so quickly. And then I didn't know if I would be welcome."

"Did they have a military draft in Britain?"

"No."

"That was your choice, then." She paused. "You can

make as many excuses as you want. And as for being welcome, you're *always* welcome to come home, son."

"It worked both ways," he replied sharply. "You could have sought me out, come over and visited."

The old woman scoffed and swept a hand around her. "With what? We lead a simple life. Even Josefa's truck still bares the evidence of your temper all those years ago..."

Lomu felt that pang of regret again. He wondered whether anybody thought about him after he had left and felt that same emotion, whether anyone had regrets about the way they had treated him or realised why he had done what he did. He doubted it. He had been unreasonable, but he had only been fifteen and full of teenaged angst when his father had died, and sixteen when his mother had started a relationship with the man that he considered a proxy uncle. It had been raw, and teenage reasoning had never been a guiding light or a beacon of common sense. "I was young," he reasoned. "And I couldn't handle the fact that you moved on so quickly."

"There are things you don't know, Davy. Things that are private."

"But we're family," he protested, then added, "Or, we were meant to be..."

"Enough," she said, turning her eyes back to the horizon. The chair rocked on, and her face lit up as the setting sun cast its rays across her. She looked on, seemingly at peace with her decision, whether he agreed with it or not. "Your father knew he was dying. We kept it from you and your sister. Josefa promised your father that he would take care of us all and that I would not be lonely or sad."

"And you just carried on. And Josefa filled in," he said bluntly. "Like a substitute player brought onto the pitch for the final minutes of the game..."

"Oh, grow up, Davy!" she snapped. "As people say today; *it is what it is*. I'm proud of you, son. I want to know more about your life and tell you all about ours, but if you can't get over this thing, this burning hatred of the fact Josefa and I fell in love and remained together, then perhaps you really should leave..." She paused. "It isn't what I want, but there it is..."

Lomu stood up, watched the sun getting closer to the horizon. "I'll be seeing you," he said. "I have to go think..."

She nodded and said, "Don't spend too much time thinking, son. The world and what's in it will soon pass you by..."

TWENTY-THREE

There was no moon, and the night sky was as black as pitch. A bank of low cloud had brought with it stifling humid air and cloud cover to blackout the stars. He had dressed in olive-coloured cargoes and a dark green T-shirt and parked his hire car up a narrow track, close to a mile further down the mountain road. The track afforded him cover and he had pulled some palm fronds over the bonnet of the vehicle for good measure.

Lomu waited outside the vehicle and listened intently. There were the sounds of the night-time rainforest as creatures either fed or evaded potential predators. Insects, arachnids and reptiles scuttled over dried leaves and fruit bats occasionally clattered through the tree canopy. The rainforest seemed to breath and pulse, brought to life by the creatures within. Although noisy as it was, he listened for the unmistakable sound of human presence. A footstep, a cough, a scratch.

Nothing.

Lomu reached inside the car and retrieved a litre bottle of chilled water. He unscrewed the cap and started to drink.

It took several attempts and a few gulps of air, but he eventually drained the entire bottle and placed the empty bottle back inside the car. Fully hydrated, he stepped onto the path and made his way back to the road and the climb towards McGregor's estate.

He could feel the heat rising from the tarmac, the moistness of the dank rainforest hemming him in. With the heavy cloud and the humidity, it felt at least ten degrees hotter than it had been that day. His eyes eventually adjusted to the gloom, the occasional glimpse of stars glinting through parted cloud aiding his progress. At about four-hundred metres from the property gates, he stepped into the forest and continued in the same direction to make certain that he avoided the CCTV mounted on the gate. He met the wall around a hundred metres beyond the entrance, and he looked for a suitable tree to climb. There were several with branches overhanging the wall. It was poor security, but he had noted the fact when he had been driven in earlier that morning. He found the right tree, a eucalyptus – smooth bark, many boughs and a towering entity over a hundred feet high – and started up the trunk to the first branch, which afforded him a sturdy platform from which to climb higher and then work his way out along the branch and over the fence. The problem now was not so much as getting into the property, but the height from which he would have to drop. He could barely see the ground in the gloom, but estimated it was fifteen feet or more. At eighteen stone, his velocity could affect his ankle and knee joints, but at least with his six-four frame, and long arms – a boxer's reach – he could dangle and lessen the height considerably. He edged out further on the branch, then laid down on his stomach and edged both legs over the branch and started to lower himself until he was hanging at full arm's length. He took a breath and let go. The fall was greater than he had anticipated, and he felt his stomach lurch and a rush of wind on his face, until both feet hit the lawn and he tucked and rolled and rested still while he took stock. When he got to his feet, both ankles were stiff, but he walked out the stiffness, keeping close to the fence and his eyes on the silhouette of the house, a faint light against the darkness, some hundred metres or more across the exposed ground.

It was 3 a.m. The time when the sleep biorhythm was at its deepest. REM, or rapid eye movement sleep. Commonly known in the military as ambush time. No lights were on within the house, and Lomu found the shortest path towards the house and took it at a walk. To a casual observer, rapid movement drew the eye. He reached the shrubbery surrounding the house and made his way around to the pool, where he'd noted that there were no security cameras, most likely for privacy, and the duo bifold doors showed no signs of being alarmed. The gentle hum of the pool pump, the pool on a night-time circulation, was the only sound he could hear. Lomu took out his multitool and selected the knife blade. He slipped it into the escutcheon and alongside the latch bolt of the lock, then caught hold of the handle and pulled the door outwards, all the time inserting the blade deeper into the escutcheon prising the lock and pulling on the door. The combined weight and leverage eventually overcame the integrity of the lock and the door pulled open. He quickly shone a pencil torch along either side of the door jamb and was satisfied that there were no tell-tale wires or broken connectors. He walked quickly and easily through the sunroom and into McGregor's office. He had noted the PIR sensors on either side of the room. It was just a short walk to the alarm keypad in the entrance hall, and he had overcome similar systems many times in his training with the SAS, but he hesitated as he noticed that there was no red sensor light shining in the passive infrared sensors. That one red light was what emitted the invisible beam that an intruder would break to initiate the system. Without it, the system was unarmed. Lomu frowned, casting the beam of his torch around the room, then froze when he saw McGregor seated at his desk. For a moment Lomu jumped, caught off guard, anticipating that the man had a gun on him, or soon would have, but then he saw that McGregor was no threat at all. Lomu found the light switch and turned it on.

The man's eyes were wide open, and his head was still joined to his neck, but only just. During his time with the SAS Lomu had worked in Colombia advising and training government forces in anti-revolutionary warfare techniques against the drugs cartels. Part of Britain PLC's unique selling point on the world stage was to not only sell weapons but give military training. With the UK you got the full package. Lomu had soon found himself unofficially taking part in raids as an 'observer' and saw first-hand what the cartel did to informers and rival gangs. He had seen what a chain saw could do to a person, but the weapon that had killed McGregor was no Oregon or Stihl, and amongst the jagged cuts, a single shark's tooth had snagged on the man's vertebrae and pulled free. Lomu stared. He had come to the man's house to find evidence of his corruption, to take an item that could prove that Kintoto Point was indeed sacred ground, but the man was now sitting dead in his chair before him. It didn't make sense. There was no sign of the Fijian weapon of war, but with the light now on, he could see blood droplets leading back the way he had entered to the now open poolside doors. He could even see his own boot treads in the blood. His eyes went to the wall, and he saw to his dismay that the sliver of metal on the leather cord was gone.

"Hello, yes, police please..." Lomu swung around and saw Carter at the top of the stairs holding a mobile phone to his ear and a pistol in his right hand. "Yes, there's an intruder in the house! He's killed my boss with an antique weapon of war, like a club with a blade, and now he's threatening me with it!" Carter sounded desperate, but all the while he was smiling at Lomu. "I know the man, he's called Davinder Lomu. He's visiting family at Kintoto Point! Help...!" Carter fired twice near Lomu's feet and split the parquet flooring. He hung up and pocketed the phone. "Oh, the shit is about to hit the bloody fan for you, *nigger*..." he grinned, and pulled the sliver of metal out from his collar, letting it dangle on its leather cord necklace. "Looking for something? When the police get here, you'll be lying dead with that Fijian sword thing beside you, and it already has your prints on it from earlier. You stole the other half of this piece of tribal tat from the church on Uluwula, and nobody will ever find this half. It's over, and your peasant family will have to go on welfare in the city, while I take over the development, as is my legal right according to the clause leaving certain business interests to me in McGregor's will..."

"Mustafa and Monique got too close to discovering what you were up to, didn't they?" He paused. "That's why you killed him. What the hell did you do with my sister?" he growled.

"Oh, my... you really don't have a clue, do you?" he laughed. "Well, that's family, I suppose. You never really get to know them, I guess." He paused, shaking his head pitifully. "And I guess you never will..." Carter aimed the weapon, but Lomu dodged right, then left and the gunshot rang out and Hemingway's typewriter chimed as a 9mm bullet went through the keyboard. Lomu darted out through the sunroom, several bullets thumping into the slate floor behind him and ricocheting in all directions, a pane of glass shattering ahead of him and a chandelier above him raining down crystal droplets. He could hear Carter screaming in rage, more bullets fizzing past his head, and he realised that the man had made it down the stairs and was in hot pursuit. A volley of bullets fizzed past his ear, a cacophony of gunshots ringing out behind him. Lomu knew that the man had used up all thirteen bullets in the Browning and was likely reloading on the run. He crossed the grass and used the darkness of the wall for cover as he ran adjacent to the house and searched for a good place to cross. He looked behind him and saw Carter crossing the lawn, illuminated by the downstairs lights. The man fired on the run, but he was firing wildly, hoping to stagger bullets along the wall. Lomu was aware that the man had been in the Australian SAS, and he had worked with, and trained them back in Hereford. The Australian army were British Commonwealth troops, and as such got the full and undiluted training. If they were Australian SAS, then they were just as good as the British. Lomu hit the deck and slid through leaves and debris, as Carter changed his aim and staggered gunshots at the other end of the lawn and back to his original firing point to cover his bases. The bullets came close to Lomu, but he'd got down in time. As Carter fired, he got back to his feet and continued to run. He used his height to leap and climb the wall, cutting his fingers on pieces of broken glass bottles that had been placed in the cement along the top of the wall. He cursed and caught hold of the additional four feet of wire mesh fence and continued to climb, but the fence made a rattling noise and bullets soon came too close for Lomu's liking, and he cartwheeled the fence and fell down the other side. Summoning all his strength and will, he struggled to his feet and limped through the undergrowth, using nothing but the gradient for navigation.

After ten minutes of trudging through the rainforest, the heat and dampness enveloping him as he swiped vines and palm fronds aside and thankful that the island only had a single species of boa to contend with and no venomous snakes, Lomu reached the road, just in time to hear the sirens and see the lights from the police 'blues and twos' as they responded to Carter's call. He threw himself down onto his stomach and ducked his head as several police vehicles and an ambulance shot past. Carter had done a number on him, and he could see no other play than to call Shabnam. But he would have to be careful. He had never fully trusted the police. That had come from being a sizeable black man on British streets. He had battled with it from the day he had landed at Portsmouth in the recruitment ship. The British Army hadn't been the beacon for equality back then, either, and the way he had been treated by the British police had given him a healthy wariness of anyone working in law enforcement, and now that there was going to be some serious heat on him, he could not take the female detective's support for granted.

Lomu stayed off the road for much of the walk back to his car. He was able to traverse between hairpin bends by sliding down embankments, although some were steeper than others and he had to run the open stretches of road, making sure that no cars were approaching before undertaking each sprint. When he finally reached the car, he quickly downed another bottle of water, tepid but thirst quenching, nonetheless. The shotgun rested where he had left it on the backseat. He took it out and loaded it, before returning it. Part of him wished he had taken it with him, but he hadn't wanted to break into McGregor's property carrying a weapon, and he knew that it could have been a very different outcome had he been armed, and that may not have been a good thing, despite what he felt for Dan Carter. No good would have come from breaking in and killing Carter.

He would have to be cleverer than that.

TWENTY-FOUR

Hire cars were easily traced. Although the credit card he had used belonged to MI5 and would show on any checks as being registered to *Monarch Assurance*, he had still had to provide his passport details and fill out the required forms at the rental company's desk. The police had only to run the most basic of checks to discover the licence plate and put out an APB – or all points broadcast – for every police officer on the island to be on the lookout for his numberplate. After an hour of trawling the streets and carparks, he found an identical white Jeep Compass and using his multitool, had the plates swapped in under ten minutes. It would be enough to buy him some breathing space. He then drove to an isolated spot on the coast, checked that he had a signal and made the call. Shabnam answered on the second ring.

"Where the hell are you?"

He ignored her question, but not her tone. A shitstorm had just descended on the normally quiet Pacific Island. "Like I'd tell you..."

"You can trust me, Lomu."

"How bad is it?"

"Bad." She paused. "They have the weapon, and there's only two sets of prints on it. One of them belongs to the late Sebastian McGregor of McGregor Enterprises. Now, I'm not a betting person, but I'd bet that if we had a copy of your prints, we'd know exactly who that second set of prints belongs to..."

"I can't deny it," he replied. "I was there, you know I was. You met me on the way out. McGregor showed me that weapon. I held it."

"And a jury will be presented with the belief that you held it right up until you almost took McGregor's head off with it." She paused. "But that's not the worst of it. The weapon has just been found in your sister's house. All of the properties at Kintoto Point have been searched."

"But I'm no longer staying with Marie..."

"But you were, and as far as I'm aware, you haven't checked into a hotel just yet, so the fact that you're packed and are on the move will look like you were trying to leave the island. Hell, maybe you're at the airport right now... in which case, I'd advise you to get away from there immediately..."

"I'm not, but thanks."

"What's the plan?"

Lomu sighed. It wasn't looking like he had one, but he had an itch he couldn't scratch. Something that Carter had said. "I need to check something first, then I guess I'll meet you and talk about what I should do next."

"McGregor has people in the police department on his payroll, I'm not sure I can protect you..."

"McGregor doesn't have anybody on his payroll," he replied. "But Dan Carter on the other hand..."

"Carter?"

"He's as bad as they come, and he's managed to get a clause into McGregor's affairs somewhere that means he's the next director of the board. He's played McGregor, just like he's played me. Now he has a patsy for his boss's death, and it looks like the development will go ahead once the dust settles."

"You'll be caught sooner or later," she said sombrely. "It might be better to make the first move and hand yourself in and state your case, along with your suspicions of Dan Carter."

Lomu thought for a moment, then said, "There's something I have to check first."

TWENTY-FIVE

He hadn't slept much, just a few catnaps really, but he had waited until dawn in what militarily, he would have called a lying-up-place, or LUP. The sun, as ever shone on Kintoto Point first as it cleared the twin mountain peaks and he remembered what his father had said about their home, *"This place is blessed because the first light of day is trapped by the mountains, but when the sun breaks free, it shines on Kintoto first, and for the longest..."* Lomu smiled at the memory. He had been gathering the nets, ready for his father to paddle them out to the reef. It had barely been light enough to see the whites of his father's eyes, but his father had stopped paddling a quarter of a mile from the shore and turned the canoe around so they could both see the sight of the first golden shafts of light piercing the gap between the mountains, and sure enough, they had watched their village cast in the golden hue, long before anywhere further up the coast, and because of the mountains, long before the towns and villages to the south.

There was no sign of a police presence at the point, and he noted that there were men already starting work at the development. The fact seemed significant. Dan Carter wasn't wasting any time. From his vantage point high up the mountain at a lookout spot he had often used as a child – an area of salvation during those tumultuous years of puberty where he could lay and think, and later kiss and fondle with his first girlfriend and drink warm beer and attempt to smoke without choking with his friends – he could see the first of the villagers heading out in small boats and canoes. Marie's lights switched out; the village now enveloped in sunlight. He could see her Suzuki SUV parked outside, and he watched as Kalara wandered out holding her younger brother's hand. Marie followed, kissed her daughter, then picked up her son and spun him around, kissing him tenderly on the forehead before handing him back to Kalara. If that didn't look like a goodbye, then he didn't know what did. He got to his feet and brushed off the leaf litter and debris as he made his way back down the narrow path to where he had parked the Jeep. He knew the old road from memory, thankful that development had not yet sprawled up the mountainside like it had further to the south, and he knew that if Marie set off around the same time that he did, then he would catch her up on Ocean Drive. Sure enough, Marie's SUV was up ahead with just two hatchbacks in between. He fell back, settled into surveillance mode. His bread and butter.

The words had played on his mind all night. He hadn't slept much, just allowed himself a few catnaps in his mountain hide as he had waited for dawn. Strange, but he was finding what Carter had said to him altogether more difficult to sink in than the fact he had been set up for McGregor's murder. But then again, some things are unimaginable. And some things are reprehensible.

The Suzuki took a mountain road that had lost most of

its tarmac surface years ago. Loose gravel now made the windy road a challenging drive, but Marie took it on with what Lomu guessed was well-practised abandon. Without the two cars between them, he was forced to drop back further, but he was on borrowed time. Marie would surely see him soon, and then it would play out a lot differently. He was still to gauge how to proceed, but he would know it when he saw it.

And then he did.

Marie increased her speed, the little Suzuki winding through the turns with typical SUV body roll and its tyres struggling for grip on the surface. Vehicles with off-road pretensions only coped with the terrain at low speeds. Four-wheel-drive and tread-heavy tyres wasn't a licence to tear up the rules of physics, and Marie found out the hard way on a particularly sharp bend beside a perilous-looking drop. The Suzuki understeered and ploughed straight ahead, its tyres sliding in the gravel, its wheels locked tight as she broke excessively. The front end crumpled, but not before tearing through the barrier. The vehicle teetered on the edge of the precipice, its front wheels hanging in the air. Lomu pulled in behind her and put on his hazard lights as he got out. Marie looked at him through her open window as he approached, her vehicle rocking gently. Even though the vehicle was only a third of the way through the barrier, the weight of its engine had found the counterpoint. Marie didn't need to know a damn thing about physics to know she was in a dire situation.

Lomu peered through the window and said, "Don't move a muscle..."

"Really...?" she said, her tone laced with sarcasm.

Lomu saw that the food she had been carrying had hit the windscreen, and rice, beans and fish dripped into the footwell, which was loaded with bottled water and toiletries.

"Where is she?" Lomu asked.

"You're not going to help me?" she stared at him indignantly. "You're so cold..."

"That's irony right there," he replied. "Did you kill Mustafa?"

"Of course not!"

"Then what happened?"

Tears rolled down her cheeks as she shook her head in bewilderment. "Dan Carter," she replied emphatically. "He approached me. He said that Mustafa and Monique were *playing Scooby Doo*..." She shook her head at the memory, visibly finding it difficult to recall, or perhaps painful, Lomu could not tell which. "He said we were going to be evicted from Kintoto Point and there was nothing we could do about it, but he would solve mine and Jake's money worries if I got Mustafa and Monique to stop being warriors for a lost cause..." She looked at him, her eyes wide with anger. "Don't stand there judging me! It's easy for you, you got out and lived a wonderful life travelling the world and seeing new things! I stayed, I looked after mom, and helped with their money problems, and when I thought it was finally done, that Kalara had grown enough for me to get my life back, I got pregnant again and then Josefa got diagnosed with cancer and I had to be there for everybody all over again!" She shook her head. "And then Jake got in trouble trying to stop the development and got sent to prison. Now, I have to support everyone!" She started to sob, and the vehicle perceptibly rocked with her movements.

"Where is she?" Lomu asked without sympathy.

"Three bends further up the hill, first turning on the right. It's an old disused hunter's cabin."

Lomu nodded. Domesticated pigs had escaped over the years and turned feral. They had also developed a taste for sugar cane and had to be hunted voraciously in the seventies before the crop was wiped out. "You're holding her prisoner?"

"No!" she snapped. "Nothing like that. I tried to stop them investigating, but Mustafa found a necklace that he said was important and there was no stopping him. When McGregor found out about it, he sent Carter to negotiate a price. Mustafa wouldn't sell it. He was adamant. Carter took out this wicked-looking club with a bulbous end. Mustafa fought with him, even landed a few good punches, but Carter swung the club and he poleaxed Mustafa right there and then." She sobbed, tears welling up in her tired-looking eyes. "The poor boy was dead before he hit the ground..."

Lomu thought about the swelling on Carter's left eye, the split skin and bruises on Mustafa's knuckles when he had seen him in the morgue. He had seen the weapon, he was sure he had, fixed to the wall behind McGregor's desk. Carter must have cleaned it and placed it back after killing Mustafa, probably enjoying knowing that the murder weapon was hiding in plain sight. "And this was on the mountain?"

"Yes."

"But if Mustafa wouldn't give up the necklace, then why on earth would he go there to meet Carter?"

Marie stared straight ahead, her eyes unblinking. "Because I set up the meeting. Mustafa thought he was meeting Monique at a quiet, secluded spot. He was sweet on her..."

Lomu's shoulders sagged. He felt for the poor lad. Lured and double-crossed by someone he would have considered to be his extended family. "So, how did Carter get hold of the necklace?"

"Talisman. Mustafa called it a *talisman*." She corrected him. "He wore it around his neck to keep it safe and vowed never to take it off until he found the other half, which he said he had already seen at the church in Uluwula. He was planning on going back there to get it. He was convinced that was all the evidence he needed to halt the development..." She sobbed and wiped her eyes with the back of her hand. "Afterwards, I thought if I could make it look like a murder and kidnap, then it would keep the case open. I already knew that Carter had killed Mustafa, so it was just a case of setting him up for the kidnapping. But..."

"It's difficult to set somebody up for a crime..." he ventured. "Especially when that person has paid off police officers and local government." He looked at her with a little empathy, despite being used himself. "So, you knew who killed Mustafa, and by your own admission, you know that Monique is safe and well. What did you hope *I* could bring to the party?"

She shrugged and said coldly, "You spent twenty years as a soldier. I thought you could kill Carter and McGregor and then Monique could turn up with a story about how she escaped, having been held against her will by them both." She looked at the sliver of metal hanging from his neck on a leather cord. "I never expected you to play detective, nor actually find the other piece..."

Lomu wished he could take credit, but he had Shabnam, and a young woman once abused by Dan Carter to thank for that. He held up his phone and switched off the record function for her to see. Behind him, a Holden pulled in, followed by a police-liveried SUV. Shabnam had been quick, responding to the text he had sent before following her. "I can't believe you put mom and Josefa through thinking they had lost their daughter..."

"I know, I'm so sorry..."

Lomu took out his multitool and used the blade to slash her seatbelt, which was both taut and locked. He opened the door and pulled her out, and quite undramatically, the vehicle was countered and stopped rocking.

"I'm not recording, but I want you to be straight with me."

"OK, I will be," she replied, almost looking relieved to have unburdened herself. "I promise."

"That night at the cookout..." he ventured, his eyes watching hers for just a flicker, a tell that would give her away. "You left just before the trucks mowed everything down. When I brought mom into the house, you were on your phone. You later redialled and got through to the emergency services."

"That's right."

"Were you calling Carter?"

"I was trying to call them off..." she sobbed. "I had no idea they would go as far as they did..."

He nodded but said nothing. There was nothing more to say. He walked her to Shabnam and handed her the phone. "I've recorded our conversation and my password is a wholly unoriginal zero, zero, zero, zero," he said. "And despite everything, she thought she was doing the right thing. If there's a chance of bail, I will cover it." Marie simply stared at the ground, humiliation and guilt enveloping her. Lomu continued, "Monique is further up the hill in an old hunter's hut. I'd like to go and introduce myself, take her back to mom and Josefa. Perhaps you can allow us a couple of hours before you interview her back at the Point?"

Shabnam looked at Marie and asked, "Is she okay?" Marie did not look up and simply nodded, starting to sob. "Alright, but I'll see for myself, then leave you both to it." She checked her watch and said, "Two hours from now, at Kintoto Point."

Despite everything, Lomu hugged his sister as she was put in handcuffs, then led gently back to the police SUV. Shabnam got back into the Holden and followed Lomu up the hill and along the road to the hunter's hut. It was a ramshackle of a building but had a good tin roof and looked watertight despite the many different size and coloured planks that had been patched over it over the years. Nature had threatened to take over and he imagined that in a year or two if left unchecked, it would be claimed by the encroaching rainforest.

He knocked on the door and called out. When the reply came, it was timid but inquisitive.

"I'm Davinder," he said softly, opening the door. "I guess I'm your half-brother..."

Monique nodded. "I can see the resemblance," she said. "Where's Marie?"

Lomu shrugged. "You're not in any trouble," he assured her. "But the secret is out in the open and I'm taking you back to mom and Josefa."

"Do they know?"

"I don't think they know anything..." He ushered her outside and waved at Shabnam that the girl was OK.

Shabnam stepped out of the car, just as a large, black Range Rover careened around the dirt bend and the driver opened fire out of the window with a handgun. The Range Rover broke hard, skidding on the gravel. Lomu could see that it was Dan Carter, but the Australian had struggled to control the vehicle and no longer looked set to shoot as he battled with the steering. Shabnam used her open door as a barricade and returned fire with her compact Glock 19. The windscreen of the Range Rover spiderwebbed as 9mm bullets punched cleanly through, but Carter opened fire from within, punching out the glass and raining his own 9mm bullets on the police officer. Monique screamed and Lomu caught hold of her and sprinted to his vehicle, dragging the girl behind him. He pushed her onto the ground and grabbed the shotgun. Carter was changing to another magazine as Lomu fired and peppered the door with lead shot. Carter screamed and started to reverse the Range Rover, finding room where there hadn't been any, taking half the rainforest with him as he backed out and drove away. Lomu reloaded the simple single-shot shotgun and fired, blowing out the rear window of the Range Rover. He turned to Shabnam, who was getting up unsteadily, a rose of blood at her shoulder, that looked like it was blooming in front of his eyes. Her white blouse was absorbing the blood and he strode over and tore at the material. He opened the boot of the Holden and took out a first aid kit and hurriedly unzipped it. He found gauze and pressed a wad of it into the wound as she groaned in pain.

"Go after him," she told him. "Leave Monique with me and go get that son-of-a-bitch..." She fumbled with her mobile phone and dialled. "Go on!"

Lomu nodded, picked up her Glock and she passed him a spare magazine. He reloaded the shotgun and propped it beside her just in case, then without another word, he got inside the Jeep and took off down the gravel track.

TWENTY-SIX

It was evident from the skid marks where the track met the gravelled road that Carter had headed up the mountain. Lomu knew that the Jeep was no match for the Range Rover's speed and power, but winding roads were a great equaliser. Sometimes, heavy vehicles with a power advantage required more energy to brake, whilst a smaller vehicle that may have been lacking in power on the straights, often had the advantage through corners. Lomu found this theory to hold some water when he saw brake lights up ahead after the third hairpin corner. He kept the power on, the small SUV making light work of the corners, while the heavy, powerful leviathan ahead of him had to slow dramatically for the bends, but barely ever got into its stride before the next corner. However, that was where Lomu's advantage would end. He may have been able to cope with the bends, but the vehicle ahead of him must have been twice the weight of the Jeep, and he could hardly force the Range Rover off the road with such a size deficit. Even using counterweight hard-stop techniques – driving into the vehicle's rear corner and nudging it before backing off the power and allowing the driver to over-compensate the vehicle's inertia – he knew he was at a disadvantage. There was a reason most of the world's VIPs and close protection teams chose large and solid SUVs.

Carter hit the brakes and the gap between the two vehicles shortened dramatically. But he stopped the Range Rover and got out, the Browning aimed at Lomu, who opened fire with Shabnam's Glock before Carter got the chance. Carter spun on his heel, not expecting Lomu to be armed with such a weapon and he leapt back into the Range Rover and all four wheels spun gravel into the air as he planted his foot on the accelerator and the behemoth slewed onwards. Lomu followed suit, but this time the gap was down to just a few metres and he risked a nudge with his front bumper, but nothing really happened and the Range Rover absorbed the impact, then gained on the Jeep steadily. Lomu kept up the pace until a sharp right-hander near the top of the peak, when the Range Rover slowed suddenly, forcing him to hit the brakes. Two pick-up trucks came around the Range Rover from the other direction, both loaded with men carrying machetes and pitch forks. Lomu suspected them to be sugarcane workers, but one of the men looked at Carter and nodded, then pointed at the Jeep. Lomu saw a couple of shotguns hastily pulled out and jostled into position, and he floored the accelerator and fired a volley from the Glock as he sped past. One of the men holding a shotgun fell back into the bed of the pick-up and the rear window behind the driver smashed into pieces. Lomu switched the pistol to his left hand and fired three shots out of the passenger window at Carter as he sped past. Carter ducked, then hastily fired a return volley. The pick-ups turned around erratically in the road and Lomu found himself switching from the hunter to the hunted, with the three vehicles now racing after him.

The Glock was empty, and he fiddled with a magazine change as he wound his way down the mountain road towards the coast. He knew where the road would take him if he allowed it to. He could either head towards Lu, a coastal village popular with tourists in search of pearls, with willing free-divers eager to dive down in just goggles and fins in search of oysters that could yield them a bonus if a pearl could be found, or he could take another turn to the Devil's Leap – a precipice of sheer cliffs rising from deep water and a graveyard to a hundred vessels and doomed crews over the years. Lu would give him a crowd, and the men pursuing him would be less likely to brandish weapons or show their intent with dozens of tourists brandishing cameras and smartphones. He slowed for the turning, swung the jeep over the gravel surface and cursed when he realised that twenty years' absence had made him a virtual stranger. Lu was a tourist destination, and as such, was serviced by a tarmac road. Still cursing, he planted his foot on the accelerator as he made his way down the steep mountain road to the Devil's Leap instead.

The status quo had flipped. And this time, it was all wrong for Lomu. Behind him, the Range Rover was larger, heavier and more powerful. Dan Carter had the training, and he would know how to initiate an effective hard-stop manoeuvre. Lomu swerved from side to side, but all he could do was wait until the man lined everything up right. He turned in his seat as the Range Rover's grille bore down on him, and he fired four rounds out through the rear window of the Jeep, and the distance widened as Carter hit the brakes and ducked as a couple of the 9mm bullets struck his windscreen. Lomu slewed through the corners and almost lost control on the loose surface as he threaded through a particularly tight hairpin bend. He could see the ocean ahead of him and knew from his childhood days that the precipice loomed ahead. He had perhaps three more bends to negotiate, and then he would be at a dead end. His pursuers would know this and if they were forward thinking enough, then one truck would park across the road, and he would have no way to escape. He cursed again, a string of expletives that he would have sworn Carter would have heard behind him above the engine noise. He hated to be boxed in. It had happened to him once before in Afghanistan, and he had escaped to tell the tale, although many of his comrades had not been so lucky. He slowed again, turned and fired, and again Carter backed off. But the man followed it up with a volley of his own and Lomu heard and 'felt' the rounds striking the vehicle, several passing close to his ear before smashing out his windscreen. Lomu waited until he was through the last bend, then hit his brakes and turned and emptied the Glock through the rear window. He was out of bullets and tossed the impotent weapon onto the passenger seat as he looked at the open ground ahead, and the looming precipice beyond. He cursed again loudly for good measure.

Carter planted his foot down hard on the accelerator and hammered into the rear of the Jeep, a hard enough contact to set off the airbags within both vehicles. Lomu felt the full force of his airbag, as if he had been punched in the face by a heavyweight with a boxing glove, he reeled away, his lips feeling thick and his nose bleeding. But he did not have time to contemplate what had happened, because Carter rammed him again, and sure enough, he felt the car slew sideways. He tried to correct the skid, and inertia physics did the rest, demonstrating the pendulum effect with savage consequences. Lomu felt the car rolling and for some strange reason he held his breath as the Jeep rolled over and over and came to rest on its roof.

The world seemed to stand still, and his ears were ringing. He could hear dripping fuel and the engine 'ticking' with heat and knew that he had to get out immediately. He realised that he was lying hanging upside down, and by the time he struggled with the seatbelt clip, he heard the gunshots and the bullets impacting on the car. He dropped unceremoniously onto the tinny roof and struggled to get his bulk out through the smashed passenger window. Carter was no longer firing the Browning and Lomu suspected that the man had run out of ammunition, and as he got to his feet, he saw the first of the pick-ups pulling into the open ground.

There was nothing for it but to run.

TWENTY-SEVEN

The Australian stood in front of him, the machete in his right hand and the talisman in his left. It was swinging from side to side, like a hypnotist's pendulum, and he had a gleeful look in his eyes. He was close to the cliff edge. Five-hundred feet below him, the surf crashed on the rocks. There were few places with a break in the reef surrounding the island, but this was one of them. Two miles out, and separated by three miles of ocean, feathers of white water sprayed in the air as twenty-foot rollers peeled off and crashed down on the outer reefs and ebbed away in the lagoon. But here, on Devil's Leap, the southern swells funnelled between those two reefs and unleashed their power at the foot of the cliffs with all their fury.

"End of the road, Lomu," the Australian said, looking over the big Fijian's shoulder to where his companions had managed to regroup, some bloodied from the gunfire, but most with a look of vengeance on their faces. "You're a big, tough guy, but you'll never take us all at once."

"Maybe not. But I'll take you," Lomu replied and carried on advancing. Six-four, eighteen stone and unafraid.

He wiped blood from his brow and looked the man in the eyes. "You're a murderer. And you'll get what's coming to you..."

"I guess you could do with a weapon right now," he said, making a show of the machete in his right hand.

"Don't need one. How about I ram my fist in your mouth and rip out your tongue?"

The Australian watched the second pickup slew over the loose surface, great rooster tails of dust and gravel thrown from the rear wheels. The sound of the V8 engine caught up with them, but Lomu did not look away. Unseen, four men leapt from the bed of the truck, shotguns in their hands and the crew that had got here first were bolstered by the reinforcements and started to shout and jeer. "It's over," he said.

"The hell it is..."

"They'll be in range in a matter of seconds. They'll be able to shoot you without hitting me, and then we'll toss your body down into the sea and the sharks will do the rest. Nobody will ever find you, and nobody will care..." The man paused. "Your family have done without you for almost twenty years, I doubt they'll even notice you're gone."

The Australian tested his shoulder with his fingertips, where blood seeped from a bullet graze. At least one of Lomu's bullets had found its mark, against all odds during the car chase. For some reason Carter had used his right hand, and not the left in which he held the talisman. The machete was heavy, and the blade wobbled as the man tested the wound. The blade blocked his view for a moment, but as with things that mattered, it was a moment too long. Lomu lunged as the thick blade blocked the man's view of both him and the gathering of men behind him. Leading with his left foot and dropping his right knee,

Lomu's righthanded straight punch caught the man in the solar plexus, and his fist went around two inches deep, crushing the bone and driving the wind from his lungs. Carter dropped the machete and fell backwards, but Lomu snatched the talisman and for a second, all that stopped the man from falling was the thin leather necklace in his hands. Lomu snatched it backwards and Carter teetered on the precipice, his arms flailing wildly, before he fell backwards into the abyss.

The gunshots started at once, and Lomu felt the sting of hot lead shot on his legs as he snatched up the machete. He had nowhere to run, nowhere to hide. He could see Carter sliding down the slope below him. Not quite sheer, but certainly impossible to climb down. Risking a glance, he saw the men reloading their double-barrelled shotguns as they rushed forward to a more acceptable range. Fiji's gun laws were strict and despite its military and police being armed with the latest and greatest hardware, civilian ownership was down to shotguns and some hunting rifles with only registered collectors licenced to hold anything else. But a shotgun was as deadly as it gets when the range got down to forty metres or less, and the men were as near as damn it, deathly close.

Lomu stuffed the talisman in his pocket as he leapt over the precipice and slid down the shale cliff-face on his backside and used the machete as an oar to both slow and control his descent. It didn't work as planned and he was soon racing at a terrific speed after Carter, and perilously approaching the sheer cliff-face two-hundred feet below him. Using all his considerable strength, he dug the machete blade in deeper and the shale spat out rocks and earth in protest, the machete blade sparking like it was being hammered in a forge, and his descent slowed considerably.

His cargoes were shredded, and he could feel the loose rocks tearing at his skin. Above him, a volley of gunfire sounded like a military salute as the men fired two barrels and reloaded as quickly as they could with shaky hands and a belly full of nerves. These were not soldiers, and nor were their weapons effective now that Lomu had slid far from range. With the visible curve of the slope disappearing before his eyes, he dug deeper with the blade, then shot forwards quickly as the blade snagged and broke in half, a metallic ring of protest filling his ears. He could no longer see Carter but had missed the man going over the edge. All he could do now was hope, and as he went over the abyss, he held his breath and closed his eyes instinctively, wishing he had never answered the texts and calls, nor boarded the two-stop, thirty-six-hour flight that had brought him 'home'.

The loose volcanic rock tore at his skin, already shredding his clothes as he slid towards oblivion. The short piece of machete blade that remained carved out a trench beside him, as he pressed ever harder to slow his descent. There was only another fifty feet of slope remaining before the ominous ledge and the drop into the abyss. He could no longer hear the gunshots above him, and was well out of range, but he glanced behind him and noted he had slid several hundred feet. When he turned back, it was too late. There was nothing ahead of him but fresh air and now free from the resistance of the rocky slope, he accelerated towards the water below and threw the remains of the machete aside. Instinctively, he snatched a breath and counted. At a count of five seconds, he risked a look, snatched another breath and braced for impact, legs straight, ankles together and his arms crossed with his elbows tucked in.

The water enveloped him, but not without a terrific jolt

that tore up through his spine and knocked the breath from his lungs. The drop, close to one-hundred feet, sent him around fifteen feet into the depths – he remembered hearing somewhere that there was a limit to how deep a person would submerge after a jump and fifteen feet was about as deep as you went whether the jump was twenty-feet or a hundred, and theoretically a thousand, although that would not be survivable - and he stroked with arms and legs to the surface with an intensity that was both urgent and primal. Breaking the surface, he gasped for breath, the salt stinging his eyes, but instantly felt a weight upon him, pushing him under the surface, and clasping his head. He had thought about entering the water cut to shreds from the volcanic rock and the risk of attracting sharks, but he could already tell that this was something entirely different. He struggled to free himself but felt a raw shaft of pain at his shoulder, and at once realised that he was bleeding, the crimson cloud enveloping him. Lomu knew he had been stabbed, and that could only mean one thing – Carter had survived the fall, too.

The man had the advantage. With the Carter clinging to him like a limpet and forcing him under the surface, he didn't have to rely solely on the knife, Lomu only had seconds of air left in his lungs. He snapped his head backwards, feeling the connection with the man's face, then elbowed hard and swam downwards. When he looked up, the man was treading water and swiping the blade around himself instinctively. Lomu swam clear, surfaced for air, then swam back under the surface and clasped the man's right foot in both hands and pulled him under the surface. He continued to pull the man's leg, tucked it under his right arm and held it against his body like a vice as he swam downwards. Carter struggled and Lomu could tell that he had not managed to snatch a breath before being pulled under. He swam with all his strength, kicking ferociously with his muscled legs, and powering with his mighty left arm. He was twenty feet deep now and had to pause briefly to clasp his nose and equalise the overwhelming pressure in his ears. He felt the welcoming 'pop' in both ears and swam down further. With a final tug, he brought the man down to his own depth, clasped the man's right hand to control the blade, then kicked him in the stomach, watching the bubbles leave the man's lips. He released his grip and swam upwards, paying the man the final indignity of using his head and shoulders as a launchpad as he pushed upwards with both feet, driving Carter even further downwards. Lomu swam for all he was worth. He no longer looked at the sinking body, just stared at the light above him, the light growing brighter with every few feet of travel. His lungs felt as if they were going to split, and in an effort to alleviate the pain, he started to expel air, which had the adverse effect of slowing his ascent and when he finally breached the surface, his vision starting to fade from the lack of oxygen, he gasped and panted and spluttered, the air having never been so precious to him.

TWENTY-EIGHT

The sea was clear and deep and surged with an ebb and flow as the rollers swelled at the base of the cliff without first breaking, creating a wash that found him propelled forwards, and dragged backwards with every sixth or seventh stroke. The effect was wearisome, but regular checks of the cliff face confirmed he was in fact making progress. Waves only broke when the swells met a depth of half the swell's height or less, and at the foot of the Devil's Leap, the water was at least fifty-feet deep at high-tide. On this stretch of coastline, the deep water provided the perfect habitat for Pacific oysters, exploited by the pearl divers of Lu, only a mile around the corner. However, Lomu had tested the current and a swim to Lu was just not possible. The cliff was too high and too vertical to contemplate an unaided climb, and he was forced to settle in for a five-mile swim around the headland to Sivu, the next village up from Kintoto Point. He checked his watch for the fifth time and estimated he had taken over an hour to clear just under a mile of coastline. Not great by pool swim standards, not even good by sea swim standards, but the ebb and flow of swells made any swim here twice as difficult as any he'd ever known. But he remembered what Josefa had once told him about distance swimming. *"Keep moving, breathe steadily and never panic. Don't set a time – just keep moving and you'll get there..."*

Lomu kept stroking, smooth and steady. When he looked up to check his progress, he noticed a boat in the distance and he started to tread water, raised one arm high above the water and waved, swinging his arm from side to side and keeping his eyes on the boat. The sun was ahead of him, and he reached for the talisman hanging around his neck, then angled it against the sun and moved it to reflect the sunlight. He could not see if he had managed to signal the vessel, but he tried all angles, and soon heard the change in engine pitch and the boat changed course towards him. He continued to wave, then stopped once the boat was a hundred metres from him and used both hands to tread water. At fifty metres he smiled, relieved to see a friendly face after what he had been through.

"Shabnam called me!" Jenny shouted excitedly. "Her men found your car and questioned some men who said that both you and Carter went over the Devil's Leap!" She cut the engine and dropped the anchor twenty metres from him, and he swam for the stern and the swim platform of the speedboat. Jenny swung the metal ladder overboard and locked it in place while Lomu tread water at the stern. "You might want to get out of the water," she said. "I saw two short-finned makos about a mile back..."

Lomu decided he had been in the water long enough, let alone with confirmed man-eating sharks in the area, and caught hold of the ladder and heaved himself out. Jenny tossed him a towel, while he sat, exhausted, on the swim platform, the swells splashing over the platform and washing over his knees. He dabbed his face and dried his hair with the towel, then stood up unsteadily and stepped over the rear seats and onto the deck. The swell rocked the boat and he fell into Jenny. They held onto each other for a moment, then he bent down and kissed her. She responded, then pulled away after a few seconds.

"That was for the dolphins," he said. "Just paying you back..."

She smiled. "I'm not complaining."

"Carter's dead," he said, then shrugged. "Seemed like a thing you should know before we continued to kiss. I may have had something to do with that."

"I see. Well, I can't say I'm sad." Jenny paused. "And yet for some strange reason, I can't say I'm overjoyed, either." Lomu said nothing. He wasn't going to lay empty words on her. Carter was blood, but he was a bastard and he had abused her as a teen. He suspected as time went on, Jenny would no longer feel benumbed or ambivalent, and would probably feel pleased that the man was no longer around. He sat down on the white, faux-leather seat and took off the talisman from around his neck. "Is that what all this is about?" she asked, watching Lomu as he studied the inscription.

"I guess," he replied. "It's certainly what killed Mustafa."

"And what about Monique?"

Lomu shrugged. "She's alive and well and with Shabnam."

"Thank goodness!" she exclaimed.

Lomu didn't want to get into it with her right now. He had hardly got his own head around his sister's actions. He studied the inscription and part of an image of a multi-headed sea serpent and a mountain. Like many sentence structures, the words flowed more in the language in which they were written. Translation surely was the bastardisation of the written word. However, in Fijian it simply read:

Degei
mountain
the
light
forever

Lomu frowned. It had never really made sense, but he reached into his pocket and fished out the piece he had snatched from Carter and held it out beside the other piece. Jenny peered from behind, resting a hand on his shoulder. When he brought the two pieces closer together, they snapped shut with a resounding 'click', both pieces ferro-magnetically compatible. Neither of them expecting it, they both reacted with a jump as if snatching back from a drift towards sleep. Lomu tried to pull the pieces apart, and it took considerable effort to attract a mere glimmer of light between both sides of the talisman. The image of the mountain was complete, and nobody was ever going to deny that it was Mount Nakandua and Arisma, twin peaks between which the early morning sun always shone on Kintoto. The image on the talisman depicted this by what looked like laser beams, shining down onto a sea serpent. Degei.

Lomu translated the entire inscription for Jenny, "Degei born of Nakandua mountain and tide of Kintoto, the sun's first light, forever rests..." And then he thought about what his father had told him as a child as they had sat in the canoe, with Lomu sat among a tangle of fishing net. *"This place is blessed because the first light of day is trapped by the mountains, but when the sun breaks free, it shines on Kintoto first, and for the longest..."*

"Will this be enough?" Jenny asked softly over his shoulder.

Lomu nodded. "The authorities can't ask for more," he replied. "According to the church museum on Uluwula, the piece of the talisman that they held had been carbon dated to around five-hundred BC. Degei, regardless of whether myth or fantasy was inextricably linked to Kintoto Point five hundred years before a virgin, a carpenter and a donkey rocked up in Bethlehem and slept in a stable. I can't see Israel building a *Holiday Inn* on top of that stable, and I can't see the Fijian government obliterating a site of folk-lore, religion and heritage."

"You've done it then," said Jenny. "You've saved your family's home..."

Lomu hung the talisman around his neck on both leather cords and stood up to face her. She had the most piercing blue eyes he had ever seen, and they radiated light and the beauty of their surroundings, like a conduit of positivity. Something about her was infectious, and he couldn't remember feeling so drawn to a woman in, well, forever. He bent down and kissed her firmly on the lips, and she responded by wrapping her arms around him and pulling him closer to her firm body. He had never felt the sensation before, but he felt secure, loved, protected and conversely, that he had someone *worth* protecting. It was a strange emotion, but it finally felt like he was home.

TWENTY-NINE

The sun baked down hard, heating the stony ground, the trees and the patches of grass so that he was heated from all sides, like taking a walk through an industrial oven. He had downed a bottle of water in the car, now just a few hundred metres away, he was ready for another. Lomu walked the narrow path along the headland. It was littered with empty beer bottles, paper litter and plastic waste. Paradise wasn't a given, it needed to be maintained and so many people on the island - the disaffected youths, the homeless, business owners who did not want to pay for expensive refuse collection needed to be better. He had always thought about his birthplace with a somewhat idyllic romanticism that he had realised in just a few short days, was entirely unrealistic. He didn't remember the rubbish, the sprawling developments laden with tourists and poverty-stricken shanty towns that they preferred not to see. He supposed that the island had exploded with tourism in those absent years, but he also knew that it had always been there to a degree. He had simply pasted over the facts with the unreliable memories of a sixteen-year-old boy.

He saw Josefa perched on the rocks, swells pounding the headland and throwing up spray that landed just short of the man's sandalled feet. He had cast his float beyond the swells and was allowing it to drift closer to shore where the fish took advantage of the movement in the water. The sand was disrupted by the swells to reveal tiny crustacea which were soon snapped up by small fish, which again became the prey to larger fish still, until eventually one large enough to take Josefa's baited hook completed the food chain. Lomu watched the man pull at the line, which would jolt the bait through the water, mimicking a swimming motion. Perhaps enough for a suitable fish to see the movement and strike. He remembered both Josefa and his father teaching him the technique as a boy. Josefa always fished when he had to work through something. There was no better way – the sea, the solitude, the light – if fishing couldn't clear the mind, then nothing could. And the man had much to think on. Marie had been arrested, although Shabnam was convinced the sentence would be lenient. Monique was back with her family, but their mother would not be letting her out of her sight anytime soon and Delilah, stunned that Marie had devised such a plan, was seemingly at their beck and call. Kalara and her baby brother, Yami, had moved in with them, and they were one big, happy family. Marie's actions had already been forgiven, and they looked forward to her return, sentence permitting. Things were never going to be the same, but at least the development would be halted and Kintoto would finally get its protected status. It may take time, but the future for all the villagers was looking promising.

Lomu trudged on, his flip-flops crunching on the gravel making the man turn around. He eyed up the man-mountain, then shifted along the rock as one would a park bench to someone approaching.

"Mom told me about my father." He paused. "How it was between you all shortly before he died."

"I see," Josefa said. "I'm sorry."

"Why?" Lomu stared down at him, declining the man's previous gesture to sit. "What do you care? You got mom, and you got rid of me!"

"I never wanted to get rid of you!"

"Bullshit! You got all nice and cosy with mom before the man's body was even cold!" Lomu paused. "I'm trying to get my head around it, but I just can't. She paints a picture of him wanting her looked after, taken care of, but I just don't see it. She was nothing more than a slut, but he must have been an idiot to not see you there on the side lines like a fox outside the hen house. Jesus Christ, what a fucking loser..." Josefa was on his feet in a split second, his rod discarded among the rocks. He shoved Lomu in the chest with both hands, but it was not a case of irresistible force meeting immovable object, and as immovable as Lomu usually was, and no lightweight himself, Josefa ended up making him stagger backwards. Lomu got his balance and took a step forward, his instinct always to fight, but Josefa was done, and he sat back down on the rock and picked up his fishing rod. Lomu remembered his size and the fact Josefa was not a well man, and he relaxed, somewhat ashamed he had squared back up to him, and said such things in the first instance.

"Take that back about your father..." he said coldly.

Lomu looked away and said, "Sorry..."

"And sit yourself down," Josefa told him. "Take a breath and relax. You don't fight flesh and blood."

"We're not exactly blood..."

"I said, take that back about your father..." Josefa repeated as if disciplining a twelve-year-old.

Lomu, his anger cooling to a simmer and feeling like a child again, found himself apologising. "Sorry," he said, then regaining some composure, and trying to fathom what had just transpired said, "But why would you care?"

"He was a good man, your father. I loved him." Josefa picked up his rod and pulled at the line, teasing the fish. He handed it to him and said, "Take this, Davinder. See if you can catch something for our supper." He waited for Lomu's stubbornness to recede and take hold of the rod. "I knew that your dad was dying. He didn't tell anyone, not even your mother until the very end. But he made me promise that I would look after her." He paused. "She had you and your sister to bring up, and without your father there to earn money, he was worried what would happen to you all when he was no longer here."

Lomu stared out to sea. "It all happened so quickly."

"To you, maybe. But not to me. I always loved your mother," he said quietly. "I was with her before your father. But true love is difficult to hold back. It's like the tide. It can't be stopped. Your father and your mother were like that. A surging tide. Sure, I was angry and hurt to begin with, but your dad was too good a friend to punish, and he made it up to me by being the best friend a man could have over the years. Your mother and he were so in love, and she was happy, which is all I wanted for her."

Lomu stared at him, the news prickling inside, but it made sense. The man truly loved his mother. "It must have been difficult to watch," he commented, suddenly feeling like a grown up and considering another man's feelings over his own. He just realised it was twenty-years too late. "You were always there when I was growing up. How could you stand to watch them together?"

"For love," he replied simply, and as if no further justification was necessary.

"There must have been more to it than that."

"There are different kinds of love, Davinder." He paused. "Lovers, siblings, mothers and daughters, fathers and sons."

"And you stayed around because you still loved her?"

"No," Josefa chuckled. "I stayed around because I loved *you...*"

Lomu looked at the man beside him, then stared back out at sea. He had always known Josefa in his life. The man had taught him to fish, to play football and when he turned fifteen, he had given Lomu tips on dating and checked that he knew what was safe and what was reckless in the pursuit of the opposite sex. His father on the other hand, had always favoured Marie. He had never truly made peace with it, but he had always known deep down that there had been a barrier between them. But Josefa had always been there. That had been why he had seen Josefa taking up with his mother as such a betrayal. The man had comforted him through his grief, helped make the necessary arrangements, been a constant friend to his mother, then had wheedled himself – for that is how he had seen it - into their family. Lomu had reacted badly, gone off the rails, and had then run away to spite them all. He looked back at Josefa, tears in his eyes. "You're..."

"Yes, son. I am." Josefa put his arm around him. Two men who stood six-feet-four and sitting shoulder to shoulder with each other must have measured five-feet-wide, yet as close as they were, two entire decades remained between them. "It's been a long time."

"This changes everything," said Lomu, staring out at the glare of the sun against the sea.

"It changes everything, or nothing. That's all down to you." Josefa paused. "I made myself available to you, because it was clear that your father and mother loved each other, but nobody can love a son like a father, a *real* father. We all knew that you were mine. And this way, I not only got to spend time with you, but I could be close to your mother, because in truth, I never stopped loving her and after your father passed, I was able to help her, and you and your sister as well."

Lomu shook his head. "But you never said anything."

"It wasn't my place. I had to love you from afar. But I was willing to do that, so that your mother could be happy." He shrugged. "Nobody can explain or define love, because it means something unique to everyone."

Lomu did not know what love meant to him – although he had felt a new sensation with Jenny - but all he knew was that he still loved his father, but Josefa meant more to him growing up than anybody else had. He had felt so betrayed that the man should step into his father's shoes so quickly, so easily that he had carried nothing but hate in his heart for the man ever since. And yet... as he sat beside him, he knew that it was true, knew that he loved him still. "And what does love mean, to you?" he asked, not taking his eyes off the ocean.

"To me?" Josefa considered this for a moment, then said, "Seeing the woman you loved with every fibre of your soul with the man that made her happy was both a pleasure and an unbearable torture. But it meant that I got to spend time with you. And for that, it was all worth it."

"You could have told me..."

Josefa smiled. "I watched you grow into a wonderful

young man, and I got to impart advice and show you things, that hopefully, you have found helpful in adulthood. If I told you all those years ago that I was your father, it would have caused trouble and I would have had to leave. The three of us shared a secret, and it was never spoken of again. To everyone else, I was an uncle to you. To your parents, I was your blood father and we never spoke of it again." He paused. "So, Davinder, you asked what love means to me, and I will say *sacrifice*." He smiled, this time Lomu looking him in the eyes. "Love is only worth the investment. Invest little, and it will return little. Invest everything, and your love will be strong." He patted Lomu on the knee and said, "I love you, boy. I always have, and I always will..."

Lomu squeezed the man's hand and said, "It'll take some time to get used to."

Josefa smiled. "We only have the time we have. Man's biggest mistake is thinking he has time. Not one second could ever be bought by infinite dollars. One day you simply wake up and it's the last day you'll ever have." He paused, staring back out at sea. "I guess now that you've sorted out our problems, you'll be going back to England?"

Lomu shrugged, looking back out to sea. His friend had told him that you can't go home again. But Lomu figured it was sure as hell worth a try. "No, I reckon I can stay a while."

AUTHOR'S NOTE

Hi – thanks for reading. I hope you enjoyed 'Big Dave's' story and got some insight into his character. Losing a parent and all that goes with it is a difficult time, and I found writing this story a cathartic experience. Yes, it happens to us all, but it's the shittiest time and anybody going through this has my heartfelt sympathy and best wishes.

Right, that's that. I'll be back with a tangled web of deceit, the hunt for an assassin, an eighty-year-old secret and stolen wartime gold. Sounds like a job for King...

If you don't want to miss news of new releases, the chance to win giveaways or hear about promotions I'm running, then you can sign up to my mailing list here:

www.apbateman.com/sign-up-now

As the reader you've already done your part and read this story, and I thank you for that. However, if you have the time to leave a short and honest review on Amazon, you'll make this author happy! I'm hard at work on another thriller as you read this, so I look forward to entertaining you again soon.

A P Bateman

Printed in Great Britain
by Amazon